Comeback Cagers

The Chip Hilton Sports Series

For more information on
Coach Clair Bee and **Chip Hilton**
please visit us at
www.chiphilton.com

Chip Hilton Sports Series
#21

Comeback Cagers

Coach Clair Bee
Foreword by Ernie Nestor

Updated by Randall and Cynthia Bee Farley

BROADMAN
& HOLMAN
PUBLISHERS

Nashville, Tennessee

0-8054-2100-9

Published by Broadman & Holman Publishers,
Nashville, Tennessee

Subject Heading: BASKETBALL—FICTION / YOUTH
Library of Congress Card Catalog Number: 2001035737

Library of Congress Cataloging-in-Publication Data
Bee, Clair, 1900–83
    Comeback cagers / Clair Bee ; updated by Randall and
Cynthia Bee Farley ; foreword by Ernie Nestor.
        p. cm. — (Chip Hilton sports series ; #21)
    Summary: Chip and Soapy work to sustain the morale of
their teammates while trying to change an arbitrary decision to
exclude State University's basketball team from the National
Tournament.
    ISBN 0-8054-2100-9 (pb)
    [1. Basketball—Fiction. 2. NCAA Basketball Tournament—
Fiction. 3. Sportsmanship—Fiction. 4. Universities and colleges—
Fiction.] I. Farley, Randall K., 1952– . II. Farley, Cynthia Bee,
1952– . III. Title.

PZ7.B381955 Co   2001
[Fic]—dc21   2001035737

1 2 3 4 5 6 7 8 9 10 05 04 03 02 01

JOHN P. NUCATOLA

President, International Association
of Approved Basketball Officials

COACH CLAIR BEE, 1963

The Chip Hilton Awards
"STARTING FIVE"

1997	Tim Duncan	Wake Forest University
1998	Hassan Booker	U.S. Naval Academy
1999	Tim Hill	Harvard University
2000	Eduardo Najera	University of Oklahoma
2001	Shane Battier	Duke University

Class and character on and off the court!

RANDY AND CINDY FARLEY, 2001

Contents

Foreword by Coach Ernie Nestor

COMEBACK CAGERS

Foreword

MY ONLY MEETING with Coach Clair Bee was in 1978 at the Final Four in St. Louis, but the name of Clair Bee had been prominent in my life for more than twenty years. To actually be introduced to him was a great thrill. At that time, Coach Bee was in declining health with very limited eyesight. When I shared with him that I, too, was a native of central West Virginia, however, his eyes lit up and we had a wonderful two-hour visit.

As a coach, Clair Bee built Long Island University into one of the country's premier basketball programs in the 1940s and early 1950s. His teams were known for tough defense and disciplined offense. His winning percentage is tops in the history of college basketball. In addition to establishing himself as a great collegiate coach, though, Clair Bee created an equal legacy as author of the Chip Hilton Sports series. His writings represent a significant contribution to the sports literature of my generation and were very exciting for me to read as a young person.

The circumstances and setting of the Chip Hilton books closely resembled the environment where I grew up, an area of small towns in 1950s central West Virginia. Coach Bee's hometown of Grafton and my hometown of Philippi are only thirty miles apart. Like me, Chip was a young man growing up with modest means while balancing his love of sports, his struggles to achieve academically, and his need to help his family by working. Yet these stories spoke to me in a very special way beyond this obvious connection.

Chip Hilton was not only an outstanding athlete. Coach Bee presented him as a young man with problems that many young people, athletes and nonathletes alike, dealt with then and still deal with today. Both winning and losing are present in Chip's career as a high school and college star, but perhaps even more important to Coach Bee's message were the lessons that Chip learned as an athlete. How you play the game, the choices you make as a competitor, the consequences of those decisions, the need for great perseverance in sports or in life—all are presented time and time again.

In Coach Bee's world, hard work and perseverance were always rewarded but not without struggles along the way. Around this theme, he touched countless readers, but few were able to express their appreciation for his writing. That day in March of 1978 gave me the chance to share with Coach the impression his writing made on me, and I will always be grateful for that opportunity.

Throughout my coaching career, I have on occasion referred to certain young men as being a "Chip Hilton," which for me is a great compliment. At Wake Forest from 1992 to 1996, we unquestionably had a modern era Chip Hilton. His name was Rusty LaRue. Rusty played football and basketball for four years while even competing in baseball one season. His grades were outstanding, and he was a married student whose first son was born during his senior basketball season. Rusty had all of the virtues of Chip Hilton and has achieved to a level that few expected. He spent two seasons in the NBA, one with the 1998 World Champion Chicago Bulls, and has continued to play in Europe. With his wife, Tammy, they have started a lovely family, now with three sons.

It is tremendously rewarding as a coach to see these qualities in young people like Rusty LaRue today, but I firmly believe that Chip Hilton exists in many of us as well. If you truly love the essence of sports, not just winning games or championships but all that is required to compete in athletics at any level, this book will touch you. Allow your imagination to take over and you just might see yourself. Chip's struggles and the need to challenge these struggles are the same today and tomorrow, just as they were yesterday.

Clair Bee prided himself as a teacher and a coach. He is still teaching us through Chip Hilton long after being with us.

Coach Ernie Nestor

CHAPTER 1

Knuckleheads and Bozos

CHIP HILTON heard the familiar ding of the hotel elevator. The door opened and then closed with a swoosh, followed by several hard-running strides along the hall. Then the keycard zip-zipped in the door's lock. But Chip was wholly unprepared for the smashing blow that threatened to tear the door off its hinges. He leaped out of bed and was nearly bowled over as his roommate, Soapy Smith, burst headlong into the room.

With one wild arc, Chip's freckle-faced teammate hurled a sheaf of Sunday papers on his bed. He shook the sports section of another paper in Chip's face. "Look," he sputtered. "Look!"

Chip gazed in amazement at the redhead's flushed face. The newspaper reports of State University's upset victory over Northern State the night before should have resulted in a reaction of jubilation and exultation. But Soapy's agitated expression reflected anything but joy.

"What's the matter with you?" Chip asked through blurry, sleep-filled eyes.

"Look! Look at this!" Soapy repeated, "Just look at this—"

Robert "Soapy" Smith's antics seldom surprised long-time friend William "Chip" Hilton. Soapy was a happy-go-lucky sort of a guy who somehow always found himself at the center of the latest excitement. Even when things were quiet, Soapy could sure stir things up, but always his heart was in the right place. Yet it was wholly unlike the redhead to give way to a wild, temperamental outburst on a Sunday morning—the only day of the week when school, basketball, and their jobs at Grayson's gave them a chance to relax.

Pacing back and forth from the window to the door, Soapy glared at Chip and tried his best to express himself clearly. "This! This is what's the matter with me," he managed. He jabbed a forefinger into the newspaper. "How do they get that way?"

"Who? And get what way?" Chip asked, perplexed.

"The NCAA!" Soapy exploded. "That selection committee!"

"What's the matter with them?"

"They're knuckleheads!" Soapy grunted angrily. "Complete bozos!"

"They can't be *that* bad."

"Oh, no? Well, here! Read it!" Soapy shook the paper vigorously and thrust it toward Chip as he passed by on his next pacing tour of their room. But before Chip could grasp the paper, Soapy changed his mind. "No!" he said shortly, hastily pulling the paper back and just out of reach of Chip's outstretched hands. "I'll read it. You're still half asleep. Listen!"

"I'm listening," Chip said calmly, watching his pal warily. Soapy's freckled face was flushed and his blue eyes were blazing as he stomped across the room and banged the paper down on the desk. Chip followed and peered over the redhead's shoulder. A bold headline streamed clear across the top of the sports page:

NCAA ANNOUNCES
NATIONAL TOURNAMENT CAGE SCHEDULE
Undefeated Southwestern Top Seeded

Forcefully tapping a forefinger under each word in the first paragraph, Soapy tried to remain calm as he read the fine print. "'The NCAA Division One Men's Basketball Tournament Selection Committee—'" Soapy paused and grunted sarcastically. "Huh! *Selection committee!*"

"Go on," Chip prompted, "finish it."

Soapy's voice was trembling, and he sputtered the words in disgust as he continued, "'—today released the Division One pairings for the four regional sixteen-team brackets for the NCAA National Tournament and announced that there remain only three unfilled spots.'"

Soapy paused and checked to make sure Chip was listening. Then, enunciating each word clearly and carefully, he read on. "'The committee stated that it expected the three remaining spots would be awarded to an Eastern team, a Western member-at-large, and a Midwest Conference representative.'"

"What's wrong with that?"

"What's wrong with it? Just listen to the rest of this drivel!"

"'The Eastern entry will be decided Tuesday night when Long Island University meets Wilson University in Philadelphia. Western Wesleyan, with three games to play and a record of seventeen victories and two defeats, is being considered for the at-large selection. The winner of the Northern State–A & M game on Wednesday night will be selected to represent the Midwest Conference—'"

Chip pushed Soapy aside and snatched the paper from the desk. "That can't be!" he said incredulously. "We're still in the running for the conference championship."

"Oh, sure!" Soapy rasped. "Go ahead, read it for yourself."

Chip spread the paper back down on the desk and, with Soapy peering over his shoulder, read the next paragraph.

> Northern State and A & M are tied for the lead in the Midwest Conference with identical conference records of 14 victories and 3 defeats. Both also rank high on the national scene with Northern State boasting an overall record of 20-3, while A & M is credited with 19 wins and only 4 defeats.

"Well? Go ahead, say it," Soapy demanded.

"Wait a second," Chip said worriedly with a wrinkled brow before continuing.

> Although conference champions have automatically qualified as contestants for the past several years, Thomas Merrell, chair of the selection committee, pointed out that "there is no set rule regarding conference selection. Further, it is possible to substitute a member-at-large for a weak representative to settle conference ties or clear other complications."
>
> Merrell concluded, "Based on the remaining schedule for each team, the committee feels that either A & M or Northern State will clinch the conference title with the other school finishing in the runner-up spot. The selection committee believes either school is deserving of a berth in this year's NCAA National Tournament."

It is also worth noting that State University, ranking third in the Midwest Conference and with a league record of 12 victories and 3 losses, could, mathematically, squeeze through to claim the league championship.

"Then why don't they wait?" Chip said unhappily, half to himself and half to Soapy.

"To see if we win the conference?" Soapy completed Chip's thoughts.

Chip nodded impatiently. "Of course!"

"Duh-huh! Read on. It doesn't get any better!" Soapy urged.

The chairman pointed out that State University could force the conference race into a tie by defeating the winner of the A & M University-Northern State University contest.

Such an eventuality would result in A & M and Northern State ending up with identical conference records of 15 wins and 4 defeats and necessitate a play-off game or series. Since the first round of the national tournament is scheduled for the following Monday, Merrell stated, "The delay would disrupt the timing of the entire tournament and result in a number of postponements with subsequent loss of academic time by all the teams concerned." Chair Thomas Merrell further stated that the committee did not think it advisable to risk the eventuality.

Chip paused and shook his head in dismay. "It's all mixed up," he said. "How could it happen?"

"Beats me," Soapy said hopelessly, shrugging his shoulders.

Chip turned slowly away from the desk and slumped

down on the side of his bed. *There goes everything,* he thought bitterly. *All our hopes and all our dreams* . . . .

"We're going to beat 'em, Chip," Soapy said halfheartedly.

His friend said nothing in reply. The events of the season sped through Chip's thoughts like flashback scenes from a video . . . his election as captain of the team, the team's need for a big man, his accidental discovery of seven-footer Branch Phillips in the school of forestry and his rapid development, the storm disaster that ruined the Phillipses' farm, Branch dropping out of school, the plan that got Branch back in school and back on the team.

Then there was the loss of the team's coach. Jim Corrigan had left for England to pursue a Rhodes scholarship. Coach Corrigan was granted an early start to his sabbatical, right after the Statesmen's disappointing defeat in the semifinals of the Holiday Invitational Tournament in Madison Square Garden.

Then there were Chip's personal difficulties with Mike Stone, the new coach, and the team's trouble with Stone; the illness of his boss, George Grayson; and the problems that arose when Chip took temporary charge of the Graysons' store.

And then came the worst blow of all. Tired and run down, Chip had been put on the ex-athletics list by Dr. Mike Terring, the team physician. The team's uphill fight to stay in contention in the conference race had followed. His return in time to forge an understanding between the coach and his teammates had ultimately led to the resulting synchronization of Stone's style of play with the team's own style, the Corrigan System that they knew so well. And last night, their team had achieved the impossible.

With everything clicking, they had engineered the big upset victory over Northern State University, Coach

Mike Stone's alma mater. That victory had lifted the team's morale to a new high and given new hope for winning the conference championship. Winning the title meant securing a spot in the national tournament, or so Chip and teammates had thought, until now.

"There isn't a team in the country that can beat us," he muttered.

Soapy had plopped down on the edge of his bed and remained deep in his own thoughts. He lifted his head when he heard Chip speak. "What did you say?" he asked.

"Nothing, Soapy. I guess I was thinking out loud."

"I know what you were thinking," Soapy said quickly, an understanding glimmer shining in his eyes. He paused briefly and then continued slowly, "Man, this was my last chance to play in a national tournament."

"But what about next year? We've got everyone back."

"I'll never make the team next year," Soapy said forlornly.

"Why not?"

"With all those big guys coming up from the freshman team plus Stone's new recruits? Are you kidding?"

"You're nearly as big as I am."

"Not even close," Soapy retorted. "You're a lot taller than I am, Chip. Besides, you can jump like a kangaroo, you're fast, a dead shot, and an all-American. Maybe you're not so awfully big, but there's a lot of difference between a gazelle like you and an elephant like me."

"I'm certainly not a gazelle, and you're *definitely* not an elephant. Besides, not all those freshmen will make the team as sophomores."

"These guys will," Soapy said stubbornly. "And what about this year's guys? Most of them will be back. Nope, this was my last chance to play on a national championship team. Now, thanks to those knuckleheaded bozos on the selection committee, I'll never play varsity basketball again, and you know it."

"I don't know it. But I know several more important things."

"Like what?"

"Like graduating, starting our careers, and working and helping our parents and others." Chip paused and eyed Soapy steadily until the redhead nodded in agreement.

"Second," Chip continued, "it isn't the end of the world and we've got no business sitting here feeling sorry for ourselves. Right?"

Soapy nodded again.

"Third," Chip said firmly, "we're not going to quit. We're going to do something about the NCAA Selection Committee! Starting right now!"

CHAPTER 2

Right on the Chin

SOAPY SMITH stared at Chip for a long moment. Then the scowl disappeared from his face and his old smile returned. "Great!" he said quickly. "Now you're talking. Where do we start?"

"First, we pack. Coach said to be in the lobby at twelve o'clock sharp."

"How about something to eat? It's only eleven."

"Nothing doing! We're going to eat on the plane. Besides, you're getting fat."

"Me!" Soapy protested. "Me getting fat? Not me! I'm in perfect shape and I'm raring to go."

"Get going then. Let's pack up. Before we do anything, I want to find out what Coach Stone and Dad Young think about all this news on the tournament. I'll call them as soon as I get dressed."

Chip headed for the shower. Soapy gathered up his clothes and stuffed them in his red and blue team bag. Twenty-five minutes later their suitcases were packed.

Chip dialed the number to Coach Stone's suite. Soapy moved over beside the phone so he could hear the conversation too.

The telephone rang three or four times before the coach answered. Chip recognized Mike Stone's voice and wasted no time with preliminaries. "Coach, this is Chip. Did you see the story in—"

"Yes, Chip, I did," Stone interrupted. "Dad Young and I are sitting here talking about it. Can you come up?"

"Yes, sir. I'll be right there."

Soapy nodded vigorously in approval. "That's the ticket! Now we're getting some action. I'll take our gear down to the lobby to save you some time."

Chip nodded and took a quick look around the room before grabbing his coat and hurrying out into the hall. Coach Stone's suite was two floors above, and Chip decided to save time by taking the stairs. Stretching his long legs, he took the steps three at a time.

The door of the suite was open. Coach Stone and Dad Young, State's director of athletics, were sitting at the small dining room table in chairs facing each other. Chip noticed the opened newspapers and pads of paper scattered on the table. The expressions on their faces were serious. Mike Stone got to his feet, motioned to an empty chair at the table, and closed the door.

Dad Young's big, heavy body filled his chair, and he made no effort to rise. But he smiled warmly and stretched out a long arm to grasp Chip's hand. "You were great last night, Chipper," he said heartily. "How do you feel this morning?"

"Fine," Chip said. "That is, except for the news about the NCAA tournament. Can't something be done about it?"

"I'm not sure," Young said thoughtfully. "Our overall record isn't very good, and we're currently third in the conference."

"I don't understand why they were in such a hurry to announce the tournament selections," Stone said bitterly.

"It sounds like March Madness may have struck the committee," Dad replied. "At any rate, Easter comes early this year, Mike," Young said gently. "They wanted to complete the games before most schools take their spring breaks."

"It isn't fair," Stone said fiercely, taking a turn pacing across the room and back. Chip smiled grimly. Coach Stone's movements echoed Soapy's travels around their own hotel room earlier that morning.

Chip sized up the coach as he waited for the next move. Stone's face was flushed, and the redness extended to his forehead and on up to his thick black hair. There was no doubt he was upset. The coach was a good six-five in height and weighed around 220 pounds. Right then he looked taller and heavier. Chip guessed it was because he was carrying himself so aggressively and taking such long strides around the room.

Stone stopped his pacing and placed his hands on his hips. "This is the first time we've been at full strength all year," he said irritably. "What a rotten break!"

"There must be something we can do," Chip urged.

Stone nodded grimly. "There's got to be," he said shortly. "Dad said he'll contact the conference commissioner tomorrow morning. That might help. There isn't much you or I or the rest of the team can do except win games. And win the conference title."

"That's the most important thing of all," Young agreed quickly. "We can't let this thing get the best of the team. A letdown now is definitely not what we need. It would be disastrous."

"Then you think there's a chance?" Chip asked.

"We can surely try," Young said.

"Getting us a chance is *your* problem, Dad," Stone interjected. "Chip's job as captain is to keep team morale high, and I've got to come up with something different for each game, some strategy we haven't used."

"It's a tough spot for all of us," Young said ruefully. "I don't know whether the commissioner can do anything with the selection committee or not, but I do know we've got to win the next three games."

"We'll win 'em!" Chip said firmly.

"It will take some doing," Young said doubtfully. "Beating Southwestern on their own court would be the collegiate basketball upset of the century. It would compare to Notre Dame's upset over UCLA."

"The team can do it!" Stone said confidently. "If we can just keep 'em up—"

"Don't worry, Coach. We'll be up," Chip declared. He hesitated briefly and then continued slowly, "We're really playing great ball now, Coach. Thanks to you."

"No thanks to me," Stone said quickly. "You guys have it, that's all. Right now, you're one of the best basketball teams I've ever been associated with."

"I'll go along with that," Dad Young agreed, struggling to his feet. "Well, let's get going. It's time to get to the airport for our flight."

Chip had been thinking about his teammates since Coach Stone mentioned team morale. Overcoming the effect of the selection committee's announcement wouldn't be easy. He'd better get busy. Now.

"Coach, I'll go on down to the lobby," he said. "I've got a lot to do."

When Chip reached the lobby, he glanced around for his teammates. A few were sunk down in chairs, studying across from the comforting red-brick fireplace, and others were looking at sports magazines in the rack outside the gift shop. Andre Gilbert, the team manager, was at the front desk returning the room keycards and checking to make sure the team bus was ready to go to the airport.

Chip looked for Soapy and saw him standing beside Robert "Speed" Morris just outside a ring of teammates gathered near the door to the street. Branch Phillips stood head and shoulders above everyone except a tall, slender man talking eagerly to the players surrounding him.

Chip groaned and turned away. But it was too late. The tall man had seen him. Sam Star was a sportswriter for the *Northern Times* and had interviewed him before last night's game. The reporter was the prodding type, and he was trying to make a quick name for himself by baiting coaches and players into making rash statements. Sam Star was gaining the reputation as an "in-your-face" reporter who often tried to stir up controversies to build his own career. Star had written several nasty articles about Coach Stone, and Chip had resented him ever since.

Star pushed his way through the circle of players. "Hey, Hilton!" he called loudly. "Wait a second."

Chip reluctantly turned around as the writer's long strides brought them face to face. Soapy, Speed, Jimmy Chung, Dom Di Santis, J. C. Tucker, and Branch Phillips were right behind Star.

"How did you like my latest column?" the reporter asked.

Chip calmly replied, "I didn't see it."

Star looked at him incredulously. "No? Really? Well, I can fix that! I've got a copy right here." He reached into his pocket and pulled out the newspaper clipping. "Here," he urged, "read it at your leisure."

Chip placed the clipping in his pocket and started to turn away.

But Star shifted his position and held up a hand. "Wait a minute," he said, studying Chip's face intently. "Mind if I ask you something?"

"Go ahead!" Chip said carefully.

"Did you read the NCAA story?" Star prodded. "The one about the tournament choices by the selection committee?"

Chip nodded. "Yes, I did."

"And?" Star queried.

"I don't understand."

"Come off it, Hilton. Stop fencing with me. You saw it and you didn't like it. Right?"

"That's correct," Chip countered wryly.

"So," Sam Star continued, "your big effort last night was all for nothing."

"Beating Northern on their home court is a little more than *nothing*."

Star grinned and shrugged in defeat. "You've got me there, Hilton. Still fencing with me, though, aren't you?"

"Not at all. I have nothing to hide."

"Well, then, Hilton, to put it bluntly and to the point, how do you feel about the committee's decision?"

"I don't like it."

"What are you going to do about it?"

Jimmy Chung, Dom Di Santis, J. C. Tucker, Brody Reardon, and Branch Phillips crowded closer, and Chip was quick to take advantage of the opportunity.

"We're going to win the conference title!" Chip said with authority.

"That's right!" Di Santis said loudly.

Chip noticed that his other teammates were nodding in agreement.

Star shrugged. "Well," he said in deprecation, "maybe you will and maybe you won't. But one thing is for sure! Northern State University will represent the Midwest Conference in the national championships."

"That remains to be seen," Chip responded quietly.

Sam Star's eyes brightened. "Oh!" he said eagerly, baiting Chip. "So you *are* going to do something about it. What?"

Chip didn't have to answer that question because, just then, Coach Stone and Dad Young stepped out of the elevator and into the lobby. Star immediately transferred his attention to the two men.

"Hiya, Coach. Hiya, Mr. Young," Star greeted them brightly. "I've been waiting to see you two."

"We're in a hurry," Mike Stone said brusquely.

"One question," Star persisted. "Are you going to protest the selection committee's decision to award the winner of the Northern State–A & M game a spot in the national tournament?"

"Of course not," Stone said sharply. "But," he continued grimly, "I can guarantee you right now that State University will win the conference championship."

"We'll kill 'em!" Soapy said loudly. "All three of them!"

The redhead's statement was followed by a murmur of assent from the players who pressed around Star and the coach.

"How about Southwestern?" the savvy sportswriter asked.

"We'll beat them too," Stone said shortly, moving toward the door. "Come on, men. Let's go."

Sam Star grabbed Dad Young's arm and walked along beside him.

"How about it, Mr. Young?" he queried. "Are *you* going to do anything about it?"

"I expect to call the conference commissioner," Young said slowly.

"What can the commissioner do?"

"I really don't know, Mr. Star," Young said coldly, releasing his arm from the reporter's grasp. "Good-bye," he added, striding toward the team bus waiting at the curb.

"The commissioner can contact Tom Merrell, the selection committee chairman, can't he?" Star called after Young.

Chip and Soapy were right behind Star. Soapy clenched his fist and shook it angrily. "*I'll* contact Mr. Merrell if I ever see him," he blustered. "Right on the chin!"

Star swung around, triumphantly seizing the opportunity he'd been hunting for. "Thanks, Smith," he said archly. "I'll print that!"

CHAPTER 3

A Second Home

STATE UNIVERSITY'S chartered team bus was warm and comfortable. The only notable indications of the winter season were the growing accumulations of road salt splashing on the sides of the bus and the snow-dusted businesses, houses, and mall parking lots steadily streaming past the windows en route to the airport.

All the players took window seats and immediately opened books or plugged in their earphones for the ride to the airport. Soapy had swung his legs into the aisle and noticed Chip staring out the window. Soapy longed for the snack he had missed at Chip's insistence but then looked down at the small bulge easing over his belt and shook his head. He looked around at his relaxing teammates and plunged his hand into his coat pocket, pulling out a giant red apple left over from the breakfast buffet. He was halfway to the core when the bus pulled up to the curb in front of the doors opening to the United Airlines ticket counter.

After all the Statesmen had checked in and made their way through security and down the concourse to the gate, Chip surveyed his teammates. A few had lingered, pausing in shops, and some were reading in seats near the gate. The rest of the squad and team managers were laughing and joking as they passed the time before their departure. It was a good sign.

Chip glanced at Soapy. The redhead usually took the lead in these extracurricular excursions, but he was having no part in the fun today. Instead, Soapy was seated away from his teammates, by the window, looking out toward the plane parked at the jetport. Soapy's unusual behavior meant he was busy planning ways and means around the selection committee's decision.

On the bus ride to the airport there had been some talk about the national tournament. But, as far as Chip could discern, there was no letdown in morale. His teammates weren't discussing it, but he could sense the inner resolve of each and every one of their hearts. They were thinking ahead to the next three games. They were determined to win, emerge conference champions, and prove State University's right to an NCAA invitation.

Coach Stone had said Chip's job was to keep team morale high. That was a captain's responsibility, and he was going to work at it. But that wasn't all he was going to do. He was determined to do something to persuade the selection committee to hold off its decision until State had won or lost. *No, that isn't right,* he reflected. Winning demanded *positive* thinking, and he intended to do something to persuade the committee to wait until State had *won* the conference title.

"Cara is going to meet me at Assembly Hall," Soapy said abruptly, breaking in on Chip's thoughts. "Mr. Grayson said he would be there too. And—" Soapy paused and regarded Chip smugly.

"And what?"

"*And,*" Soapy continued pointedly, "Mrs. Grayson and *Mitzi* will be with him."

"What's that supposed to mean?"

Soapy grinned. "Who are you kidding, Chip?"

Chip felt the slow burning flush creep over his face, and he straightened up in his chair and cleared his throat.

"If you're trying to draw my attention to the fact that Mitzi will be along," he said emphatically, "you can forget it! She means nothing to me."

"Of course not. Why, you hardly know she's alive," Soapy teased.

"That's right!"

Soapy eyed Chip for a moment and then swiftly changed the subject. "When do we start doing something?" he asked meekly.

"Right now," Chip said, reaching into his pocket for a piece of paper. He pulled Sam Star's newspaper clipping out and glanced at it briefly. Then he crumpled it in his hand and tossed it into the nearest trash container.

"Aren't you going to read it?" Soapy asked curiously.

"Nope," Chip said decisively. "I don't want to read anything he writes. Ever! Right now, we've got to concentrate on making the NCAA Selection Committee wait until we win the conference title to make decisions. There's one thing that worries me though."

"What's that?"

"Remaining anonymous."

"You mean like working undercover?"

Chip nodded. "That's exactly what I mean. And while we're on the subject, no more making derogatory remarks to reporters."

"I wasn't talking to that Star guy!" Soapy protested.

"Not directly maybe. But he's the kind of reporter who likes to twist things around, and he could use your words to make State and all the rest of us look like sore losers."

"Man, I never thought of it that way. Me and my big mouth!"

Soapy grabbed a pencil and some paper from his carry-on and settled back in his chair. "All right," he said, "you call off the ideas, and I'll make like a secretary."

"First," Chip said thoughtfully, "we've got to contact the University papers."

"We'll go right to the top," Soapy said aggressively, "to the sports editors. Bell and Locke both like you, and they're in State's corner. All you have to do is drop a hint to them. And they'll move fast. That way we'll hit everyone in University and all over the state. Right?"

Chip nodded. "And next we've got to reach the national print news services and the Internet news groups—especially the ones that have Web sites."

Soapy jumped in. "Bill Bell and Jim Locke could do that easily enough. The Associated Press and the others could really be helpful," Soapy repeated. "You'll give the word to Bell and Locke, right?"

"Right," Chip agreed. "Now we come to the basketball writers from the big cities. That has me stumped. I don't know how to go about it."

"Gil Mack writes for the school paper, and he's a good friend of mine," Soapy said tentatively. "He's crazy about basketball, and I'm sure he'd love to help. Besides, he's got the means to get out the news releases. And he can reach the basketball writers through their online columns."

"Good idea," Chip said cheerfully. "I'm sure Dad Young will utilize the State University web site too. That leaves the radio listeners and some of the school's prominent alumni who faithfully follow the basketball team."

"I can get Tim Hall to handle the alumni," Soapy said quickly. "Tim works in the alumni office."

"Great! And Mitzi can contact Gee-Gee Gray. She speaks to him on a regular basis since she gives him a lot of Grayson's radio advertising. Let's see now; what's left?"

"The selection committee!" Soapy said quickly. "We've got to reach *them!*"

"I'd better think about that a little more," Chip said swiftly. "That about wraps it up."

"Good!" Soapy said. "Here's the list." He rose from his chair and stretched his arms above his head. "I, er, I need to create a little excitement. Mind if I take a stroll before we board?"

"Of course not. Anyway, I want to do some studying."

Soapy strode briskly away as Chip studied the paper the redhead had drawn up. Soapy had indeed made like a secretary.

Item	Contacts	Responsibility
1	Jim Locke (*News*)	Hilton
2	Bill Bell (*Herald*)	Hilton
3	AP + Internet	Hilton
4	Basketball Writers (Mack)	Smith
5	Radio (Mitzi)	Hilton
		"And how!"
6	Prominent Alumni (Hall)	Smith
7	Selection Committee	(?)
8	State University Web site	Dad Young, Athletic Director

Chip chuckled when he saw item 5 and the notation following his name. The "and how" referred to the former love of Soapy's life, Mitzi Savrill. Mitzi was a student at State University, but she practically ran the college side of Grayson's for their boss, George Grayson. Until a short time ago, Soapy had been desperately smitten by her charms.

Then Cara Davis had been added to the staff, and the cute little blue-eyed blonde had immediately captured Soapy's heart. Now Soapy gave Mitzi a wide berth. He wasn't going to give Cara fuel for an argument or the slightest cause to be jealous. Soapy had it bad, and Cara seemed to like Soapy well enough to give him hope.

Chip folded the paper carefully and placed it in his pocket as the team lined up to board the flight to University. Once on board, seated, and buckled in, he settled down to do some reading. A few minutes later, he drowsily closed the history book and leaned back in his seat.

It seemed only a few minutes before the flight attendant shook him awake. The overhead cabin lights were on around him, and a quick glance out the window showed a dusky, cloud-filled sky. He must have fallen asleep before takeoff.

"Time to eat, Chipper," Soapy said from across the aisle. "Put your tray table down or give me your food. Most of the guys are already eating."

Chip considered briefly and then shook his head. "No, thanks, Soapy. I'll pass on the meal. You can have it."

As Soapy hurriedly finished his second inflight snack he turned to face Chip. "Well," he said, "was the list all right?"

"Perfect. We're going to be real busy for the next couple of days."

"Great!" Soapy agreed exuberantly. "What with our undercover work and school and studying and practice and work, midnight oil, here we come! We'll just sleep fast again. Ah, the life of a college student."

The flight attendants walked up and down the aisles collecting the last remnants of snacks and drinks as the captain flashed on the "Fasten Seat Belt" signs. The plane made its final approach. As the wheels touched lightly onto the runway, Chip smiled.

It always felt as though he were coming back to a second home when he returned to the college town. University's residents were friendly and strong supporters of the school and all its programs, and Chip had made many friends in the community. His real home was, of course, Valley Falls. Mary Hilton, his widowed mom, lived and worked there, and they now owned the house in which he had been born. Someday they would be together all the time, and he would do the working for the family.

The plane parked at last, and, like most of his teammates, Chip peered out the window before pulling his carry-on down from the overhead luggage compartment. As the cabin door opened, passengers lined up to exit to the warmth of the terminal.

Chip didn't realize the gate area was filled with people until he walked up the jetway and into the terminal. People waving red and blue State pennants and signs jammed the gate area. He recognized a few faces, and then a few members of the student jazz band began to play the State University fight song, accompanied by shouts and cheers by the State crowd. Travelers caught up in the spirit of collegiate athletics even joined in.

With Soapy and Speed right behind him, Chip led the way to the baggage claim, where Biggie Cohen, Red Schwartz, and their other friends from Jefferson Hall immediately surrounded them. Biggie flung a heavy arm around Chip's shoulders and grabbed his bag. "I'll take care of this, Chipper," he said exultantly. "Great win!"

"Yeah," Red added, "Really great! We listened to Gee-Gee Gray's play-by-play last night and could hardly believe it."

All around them, Chip could see fans carrying hastily prepared cardboard signs. Many of the students surrounding the signs were shouting the cheers, and it sent a warm glow surging through his heart. State fans were loyal all the way! His thoughts winged back to the team's return from the Invitational Tournament. The reception had been the same.

Two of the fans lifted a companion up on their shoulders, and he led the students in a cheer.

"Yeah team! Yeah Coach! Yeah State! Hurrah!"

Everyone around the baggage carousel joined in on the big "hurrah" at the end, or so it seemed to Chip, and the noise was so great it was hard to hear half the questions the fans were shouting to his teammates and him.

"How did you guys ever win up there?"

"What happened? We heard Stone nearly had a fight."

"Hey, Hilton! Someone said their coach tripped you."

"Any truth to it?"

"Guess you felt pretty good beating your old coach, eh, Stone?"

"And on his own court too!"

"Yeah, that hasn't been done for years."

"What are you guys gonna do about Southwestern? They've only lost one game on their court in ten years!"

Chip didn't let on that he had heard the last question, but he was thinking to himself that it had been State who had upset Southwestern, and *he* had played in the memorable game. He had been thinking back to that game ever since last night. Beating Northern State University had been a big win, all right, but upsetting Southwestern on its *own* court would be something else again. Southwestern would remember State's visit and would be looking for revenge.

The baggage carousel emptied, but the fans made no move to leave. Chip, however, began edging his way through the joyous throng. Mr. Grayson had been ill and was probably waiting at Assembly Hall.

A SECOND HOME

Soapy suddenly dug an elbow sharply into Chip's ribs. The redhead was nodding toward the back of the crowd. Chip followed Soapy's glance and saw Bill Bell and Jim Locke threading their way through the crowd, heading straight toward him. Both sportswriters were grinning, clearly sharing the enthusiasm of the fans.

"What a break!" Soapy hissed. "Go to work!"

"Don't worry," Chip said crisply.

CHAPTER 4

Sweet Glow of Victory

SOAPY BARELY had time to turn away when the sportswriters reached them. "Hello, Chip," Bill Bell said, grasping the young star's arm. "Let's get out of this mob so we can talk." He guided Chip expertly through the milling fans and toward a quiet corner of the room where it was possible to talk without yelling. Jim Locke followed.

"You fellows did yourselves proud last night," Bell said proudly. "You've got the whole state talking!"

"That's an understatement!" Locke added. "We bumbling doubters never figured you had a chance."

"It wasn't easy," Chip said.

"How about Southwestern?" Locke asked eagerly. "That'll be a little different story, eh?"

"We beat them before."

"You seem pretty confident," Bell said.

"We've got to win," Chip said.

"But Southwestern isn't in the conference," Locke observed.

"No," Chip agreed, "but they're seeded number one in the tournament."

"Listen, Chip," Bill Bell said, "we wanted to talk to you about that. How do you and the rest of the players feel about the action of the NCAA—?"

"And what about the tournament selections they've made?" Locke interrupted.

"Well," Chip said, choosing his words carefully, "we're not in a position to do any complaining, but if *someone* could put a little pressure on the selection committee so they would hold off until Saturday . . . ."

Bell nudged Locke. "And just how could these couple of someones apply this pressure you mentioned?" he asked.

"Easily," Chip answered quickly. "What State University basketball needs right now is positive publicity, which means local columns as well as press releases to the national news services."

"You wouldn't be thinking about a couple of writers from the *News* and the *Herald,* would you?" Locke asked teasingly, nudging a smiling Bell.

"Actually, I was," Chip said honestly. "Coach can't say much about the team right now. Neither can the players. And it will be too late by the time we win the conference."

"*If* you win the conference," Locke observed.

"We're going to win it," Chip said firmly. "Right now we're the best team in the country."

"I like your confidence," Bell said dryly. "You know something, young man, I'll bet there are two guys pretty close to you who think the same thing."

"That's right," Locke added. "We happen to think you just might be able to do it."

"Right!" Bell agreed. "Well, we get the message. Watch the papers tomorrow."

"And the big news services," Locke added. "We'll start

you on the sports pages, but you'll have to make the *front* page on your own."

"There's Coach Stone," Bell interrupted, pulling Locke's coat sleeve.

"Let's latch onto him before he gets away. Good luck, Chip."

Chip called out his thanks as the two men started to walk back around the edge of the crowd. But he wasn't getting away that easily. The fans spotted him and walked along, yelling their congratulations. The sweet glow of victory had followed the team home.

Another crowd lined the driveway of Assembly Hall as the State University team bus lumbered up to the main entrance. Coach Mike Stone was the first to emerge from the bus, followed by the assistant coaches and team managers. Chip led the players off the bus and saw Mr. and Mrs. Grayson, Mitzi Savrill, and Cara Davis waving from just inside the main entrance of the lobby. He started toward them. Once inside the warmth of the building, they greeted him joyously.

"Nice going, Chip," George Grayson commented, slapping him fondly on the back. "It was a wonderful victory."

"I knew you could do it," Mrs. Grayson said proudly.

"Me too," Mitzi said sweetly.

"*And* me!" Cara echoed. She grasped Chip's arm and turned him toward the smiling man who stood beside her. "This is my father, Chip," she said fondly. "He's one of your biggest fans."

"I sure am!" Landon Davis said heartily. "I've followed your career for years. I'm happy to meet you."

Chip barely had time to shake hands with Mr. Davis before Soapy pushed into the center of the circle and took over. "We had a tough time," he said dramatically. "It looked bad for us when Chip and the guys ran out of steam. I was sitting on the bench—"

"Naturally," Cara interrupted.

Soapy was stopped but only for a second. He recovered quickly and went on, raising his voice to attract as much attention as possible. "Yep!" he continued, "it looked *bad*. There we were, only two points ahead, with seven minutes to play and everyone dead on their feet. Coach always asks my advice in emergencies."

"Oh, sure!" Cara said dryly.

Soapy glowered at her for a long moment. Then, looking around to make sure everyone was listening, he went on. "Well, as *I* was going to say, Coach looks at me and he says, 'Smith, what should we do?' Well, you know me—"

"You can say that again!" Cara observed.

Soapy, determined to finish, completely ignored her this time. "'Well,' says I, 'Mike' . . . er, 'Coach, I think I can do it all by myself.' Ahem!

"So I go in and I take three tough jump shots, and I sink 'em all. Every one of those shots was a masterpiece, if I do say so myself. But those pesky Northerners caught up and so I took another shot. And guess what? Again, I drilled the net. Well, you know what happened next. Yep, those pesky Northerners caught up again.

"Right then and there, I made the big play that won the game. With the score all tied up, 70-70, I drove in to the basket. I was going at full *gazelle* speed, you understand—"

"A mile an hour," Cara said.

"A mile an—" Soapy stopped and glared at Cara. Then he glanced around at the appreciative circle of faces and raised his voice a bit more. "As I was saying, I was moving at full *gazelle* speed, and there was only a second to play. So I took off at the free-throw line and I floated through the air—"

"With the greatest of ease—*please*," Cara added.

Soapy tried again. "I floated through the air and I dunked the ball, and then the game was over. Now I'm a hero!"

"Let's give the hero a big cheer," Cara said sarcastically.

"Aw, Cara," Soapy began, "I, I did it all for *you*—"

Cara laughed. "Wait a second. I want to ask you something, Robert 'Soapy' Smith. How come State University lost all those games when Chip was sick? Especially with you around to help Coach Stone?"

"Why," Soapy sputtered, "Coach Stone, er, Mike, didn't know how good I was, being new and everything."

"And with you being so modest," Cara added with a smile.

"Right!" Soapy agreed, beaming. "Modesty *is* my most admirable trait. Ahem!"

That broke up Soapy's story, so his teammates and their families razzed him one last time before heading out the doors of Assembly Hall.

"Shall we go?" Cara asked. "I know the players want to get going."

"Me too," Mr. Davis said. "Can I give you guys a lift?"

"We're working men," Soapy said, glancing at Mr. Grayson. "We've got to get down to the store."

"Come on then," Mr. Davis said, starting toward the doors.

"I'll take Chip in our car," Mr. Grayson said quickly.

Landon Davis and Cara took off with Soapy while Chip and Mr. Grayson followed Mrs. Grayson and Mitzi across the circular driveway to their car in the nearly deserted parking lot.

The quiet trip to Grayson's was a relief after all the excitement and celebration at the airport first and then again at Assembly Hall. Mr. Grayson must have sensed Chip's desire for quiet because he steered the conversation away from basketball and talked about the store and plans for spring instead. George Grayson parked in his reserved space in the parking lot across from the business. Chip helped Mrs. Grayson out of the car and across the street to the store entrance. Although George Grayson looked much better now, Chip could see he was still recovering from the illness that had incapacitated him a month earlier.

Grayson's, a long-established business in University, began as a small pharmacy and retail business. Mr. Grayson, a State University alumni, had purchased the adjoining buildings over the years and expanded the business to include a casual dining area that primarily catered to the college students. An avid sports enthusiast dedicated to State University, he had most recently added a wide-screen TV, a remodeled old-fashioned soda fountain area, and a small food court filled with large booths and tables.

A favorite of families, college students, and high school students, Grayson's enjoyed a strong following. Remembering his own college days, George Grayson made it a practice to employ and give responsibility to State University students in his business. Because of him, many students were able to pay their way through State University. He had also discovered a growing number of high school students who benefited from having part-time jobs at his store.

Chip was the last of the group to enter the store, but several of the customers immediately recognized him. Two of his friends, Fireball Finley and Whitty Whittemore, were behind the fountain and shook their fists in the air in jubilation. They didn't stop serving their customers, but the two were talking about Chip, and heads all along the counter turned in the young star's direction. Chip felt a thrill of pride, but it was also a little embarrassing. He excused himself and hurried on through the store to the stockroom.

Skip Miller and Lonnie Freeman, his two assistants, were filling department orders when he walked into the room. They took one glance and dropped their work. "We had the radio on all through the game. In a word—awesome, baby!" Skip said.

Lonnie kidded his partner. "That's two words, Skip. It was great, Chip! Mr. Grayson came down to listen, and everyone in the store had me running back and forth, telling them the score. I sure wish it had been televised—then we could've watched it on the wide screen."

"In the whole place, we had more people talking State University basketball than ordering food or buying things," Skip added.

"Chip, let me help you," Lonnie offered. He moved behind Chip and took his coat and team bag. "It's sure good to have you back. Hey, guess what? Skip's team beat Sheridan Prep yesterday afternoon!"

"Seventy-eight to sixty," Skip said proudly.

"Skip got thirty-one points," Lonnie added. "Bill Bell said he was a second Chip Hilton . . . nearly the same size, same color hair, same dead shot!"

"Cut it out, Lonnie," Skip said, grinning.

"Then everybody's happy," Chip said.

"Except for the national tournament," Lonnie commented reluctantly.

Skip cleared his throat. "We cut the tournament brackets out of the paper," he said hesitantly. "Did you see them?"

"No," Chip said ruefully, "but I did read about the teams."

"I'll bet Soapy went ballistic when he heard about it," Skip said tentatively.

"Worse than that!" Chip said, smiling. "He'll be here in a few minutes, so get ready for the freckle-faced whirlwind. Where's the paper with the brackets?"

"On the wall over the desk," Lonnie replied, pointing to the bulletin board. "Skip and I were going to keep the State scores."

Chip smiled briefly. "Maybe you'll still have a chance to do that."

"You think so?" Skip asked quickly. "You think it'll make a difference if you win the next three games?"

"It might," Chip said. He walked over to the desk and studied the posted brackets. Skip and Lonnie followed.

Skip reached over Chip's shoulder and pointed to the lines that were drawn under the A & M–Northern State pairing. "It isn't fair, is it?"

"No, it isn't," Chip said shortly, wanting to change the subject. "Well, what's to be done around here?"

"Nothing!" Lonnie said proudly. "We're all done. The pharmacy, retail, and food divisions are all caught up. You can call it a day. Ask Skip."

"That's right," Skip agreed. He paused and gestured toward the door. "You hear what I hear?"

"Soapy!" Lonnie cried, heading for the door.

Chip heard the commotion too—the friendly ribbing and his friend's sharp retorts. Things always happened when Soapy appeared on the scene.

Before Lonnie reached the door, Soapy had bounded in and headed straight for the desk. Without a word, he pulled a pad of paper from his backpack and began writing furiously. Lonnie and Skip exchanged glances and looked questioningly toward Chip, bewilderment reflected in their faces. This wasn't the Soapy they knew!

"What's up with him?" Skip asked.

"He's working on an important problem," Chip explained. "And that reminds me. I've got a couple of things to do myself. You guys have done a great job, so go ahead and enjoy the rest of the day. I'll see you tomorrow after practice."

CHAPTER 5

Hoop Sense and Nonsense

JEFFERSON HALL had been home to Chip and Soapy since their first day of college. The two friends shared a room in the old brick dorm that was only a few minutes' walk from the heart of the State University campus, and Soapy had worked out a morning routine that he never varied. Chip knew it by heart. His roommate would get up at 7:00, dress, set the alarm for 7:30, tiptoe out of their dorm room, and head for the convenience store two blocks away. There he would grab a hot drink as a ruse to kid around with the people behind the counter, buy a copy of the *News,* and then time his return to Jeff so he would arrive precisely at 8:00, just as Chip finished dressing.

Then, as soon as they had stuffed their books into their backpacks, they would bang on the doors of rooms 214 and 216, and Speed and Red and Biggie would join them to walk across the campus to the student union. Chip and the rest of the Valley Falls crew started every school day eating breakfast together in the cafeteria.

While they were eating, Soapy would peruse the newspaper and comment on each item, despite his companions' protests.

The procedure never varied, and this particular Monday the redhead's timing was perfect. Chip was getting his books together when he heard his pal bounding up the cement steps. A moment later Soapy raced through the door and handed Chip a copy of the *News* opened to the first page of the sports section. "It's working, Chip," he said jubilantly. "Look at the headline. Bill Bell wasn't kidding when he said he was going all out."

Chip glanced quickly at the headline across the top of the sports page. Bell had really started them off with a bang!

STATE UNIVERSITY THE VICTIM OF HASTY NCAA DECISION
Locals Eliminated from Consideration for National Tournament

The selection committee in charge of choosing the teams to compete in the NCAA National Championship Basketball Tournament (Division One) has eliminated State University from consideration. The committee cited several reasons in support of its decision to invite the winner of next Wednesday's battle between A & M and Northern State to represent the Midwest Conference.

State athletic officials declined to comment on the announcement, but it is expected that Dad Young, State's veteran director of athletics, will speak with Ned King, the Midwest Conference commissioner, this morning.

"Now read Locke's column," Soapy said excitedly. "It's great!" He leaned over Chip's shoulder.

COMEBACK CAGERS

HOOP SENSE AND NONSENSE
by Jim Locke

State's valiant basketball team, plagued all season by injuries and misfortunes, arrived back in University late yesterday afternoon. A cheering crowd of some fifteen hundred fans greeted the team at University Airport and Assembly Hall.

Fans were elated by the startling victory staged by the Statesmen's upset over powerful Northern State University Saturday night on the opponents' court.

Despite the enthusiasm, a disquieting note is causing considerable concern in University sports circles. The announcement by the NCAA Selection Committee stated that the winner of the upcoming game between A & M and Northern State University, with each team owning identical 14 and 3 records in the conference, will represent the Midwest Conference as the entry for the national tournament.

The release was disturbing! In past years, the conference title winner has represented the Midwest Association in the national classic during March Madness. The present standing of the teams finds State University in third place, with only a mathematically remote chance of gaining the title, but the possibility *is* present and *should be* recognized.

Contacted late last night, selection committee Chair Tom Merrell conceded that State University's unexpected defeat of Northern State University was an outstanding accomplishment, but then he added that the victory still leaves the Statesmen with a 17-8 overall record, which is far from sensational.

"Sure!" Soapy interrupted, "but he didn't say anything about you being unable to play when we were losing all those games."

"I played in some of them, Soapy," Chip reminded.

"One!" Soapy said hotly. "Exactly one game! Doc Terring had you sidelined for *seven straight games*."

"That doesn't mean a thing."

"Are you out of your mind?" Soapy exclaimed. "All-American players with forty-point averages don't grow on trees! Besides, Branch Phillips wasn't on the team either when we lost a lot of those games. A seven-foot center makes a big difference to *any* team."

Chip agreed with that, so he didn't debate the point. He turned back to the paper. Soapy again leaned over his shoulder to read along with him.

> The chair also pointed out that State University must play A & M and Northern State on consecutive nights this coming weekend. A State victory over the winner of the Wednesday night game would force the conference standings of these two teams into a tie, and a play-off game would then be necessary. This would disrupt the tournament schedule set up months ago (dates, playing courts, academic responsibilities) and shorten an already tight schedule, which is largely the result of this year's early Easter vacation.
>
> I would like to know what power the chair and other committee members have been gifted with that enables them to foresee the collapse of a team that I and countless others believe to be the best in the country.

"I hope the committee sees—" Soapy stopped and pondered the thought a moment. "That's it," he muttered. "That's it!"

"What's *it,* Soapy?" Chip asked.

Soapy shook his head violently. "Nothing, no big deal. Nothing at all! Just read what he says about Southwestern."

Chip turned back to the paper.

> Chair Merrell drew attention to the fact that the Statesmen must face undefeated Southwestern on the SWU court next Wednesday night and implied an almost sure defeat for State University.

"There he goes again," Soapy growled. "Wait until *we* get through with Southwestern."

"They're a tough bunch at home," Chip reminded him.

Soapy shrugged. "It means nothing," he said. "We'll kill 'em!"

Chip continued reading.

> Once more, I question the infallibility of the selection committee's predictions. Southwestern University is ranked number one in the nation and has posted a list of forty-three consecutive victories during a two-year period. That is true! And a victory over the Statesmen would mean another undefeated season. That is all true! But I would also like to emphasize that State University was the last team to defeat Southwestern, upsetting them two years ago.
>
> The present State team is a better team and, in my opinion, the best basketball team in the country as of today.
>
> Further, using my own crystal ball, I hereby predict that next Wednesday night, State (in the role of spoilers) will again ruin an undefeated season for Southwestern and snap that home-court winning streak.

> The members of the NCAA Selection
> Committee are going to be wearing some vividly
> red faces before this weekend is over!

"Wow!" Soapy said in delight. "Way to go, Locke baby!"

"Good," Chip said, rising with his backpack already slung over his shoulder. "Let's get the rest of the guys."

It had stormed during the night, but the path through the park they usually took to the student union was only partly covered with snow. The five friends settled into their familiar routine. Chip and Speed took the lead, stepping out with long strides. Soapy kept up a constant chatter with Red and Biggie.

"You're gonna see Mitzi about Gee-Gee Gray, right?" Soapy called ahead to Chip.

"Right! I've got it all written out. All I have to do is hand it to her."

"We can't let things drift," Soapy warned.

"I know."

"Have you decided what to do about the selection committee?"

"Nope."

"I'm gonna see Gil Mack and Tim Hall this morning."

"I know."

"You think Bill Bell and Jim Locke will contact the news services?" Biggie asked.

"Yep," Soapy and Chip answered in unison.

The five friends left the park and strode along the walk in front of the library. Professors and students were making their way to various classrooms and lecture halls now, and they exchanged greetings with the five.

Turning in at the student union, Chip and the others cut across the foyer to the cafeteria. Soapy headed for their usual window table with all their backpacks and then hit the serving line with the other four breakfast club members from Valley Falls. Each carried a large glass of orange juice, a bowl of hot cereal, a platter of pancakes, and a glass of milk to the table. Soapy liked this process since he also got to spend time talking with the student workers behind the serving lines. The hungry redhead took in a mouthful of pancakes and then rolled into his usual morning news broadcast.

Biggie and Red plied Chip and Speed with questions about the Northern State game, completely ignoring Soapy, who droned on and on, skipping from one subject to another, covering column after column and page after page. Soapy had no class scheduled for the first hour. When Chip and the others left at a quarter to nine, the redhead, without skipping a beat, turned to face the next table and continued his monologue.

Chip had studied every possible minute over the weekend, on the plane and in the hotel, and he was well prepared for his classes. The time passed quickly, and he finished his morning work just as the big clock on the student union tolled twelve o'clock. He cut through the park and took a shortcut to Main Street, University's most popular drive, and in a few minutes he arrived at Grayson's.

There was little action at the store counters, but the fountain, booths, and food court tables were filled. Mitzi Savrill wasn't at the cashier's desk, so he headed back to the stockroom and began filling department orders. He was still engrossed in his work when Lonnie Freeman reported for work at 3:30. Chip put on his coat and walked out through the store. He reached the cashier's desk just as Mitzi breezed in.

"You're late," Chip teased. "I've finished half a day's work already."

"Yes, and I'll have done twice as much work before you get back from basketball practice," she retorted sweetly.

"That reminds me," Chip replied, pulling the paper out of his pocket. "Could you read this and see if you can do anything about it?"

"What's it all about?"

"You'll understand when you read it. And, um, Mitzi, it's confidential."

"You can trust me," Mitzi said.

"I know," Chip said, turning away. He strode rapidly along Main Street, thinking what a great girl and friend Mitzi was to everyone. She was intelligent, pretty, and someone he could rely on. And she seemed to like him. He frowned at the thought and tried to put her out of his mind for the time being. Right now, his big interest was basketball.

CHAPTER 6

In
a Mess

MURPH KELLY, State's veteran trainer, smoothed the layers of tape around Chip's ankles and grunted in satisfaction. "All right, Hilton," he said gruffly. "Beat it! Report for practice."

He turned to Dom Di Santis and Rudy Slater, who were waiting their turns. "Well, come on, one of you," he said sharply. "Hop up here. I don't know why you fellows can't get to practice on time."

Chip winked at his teammates and walked over to a bench on the side of the training room to lace up his shoes. The tape was too tight, so he worked and twisted his ankles to loosen it. When it seemed more comfortable, he put on his shoes, laced them up, and headed for the team strategy room.

Like his predecessors, Coach Mike Stone used one of the Assembly Hall classrooms for basketball strategy sessions and watching videos of upcoming opponents. Chip's teammates were talking softly and waiting for the meeting to begin as he entered quietly and looked around. Speed and Soapy were sitting together, and Soapy was scribbling something in his notebook. Chip sat down in the vacant chair next to the redhead, who barely grunted when Chip joined him. Speed winked and waved at Chip in greeting.

A white board extended across the wall at the front of the room, and three rows of chairs faced it. Andre Gilbert, the team manager, always placed a pencil and small notebook on the writing arm of each chair so the coach's instructions could be written down.

Coach Stone was seated at a small desk at the left front corner of the room, studying a sheaf of papers. As he waited for Coach Stone to start the session, Chip studied the board. It was covered with Southwestern scouting notes.

A few minutes later, Dom Di Santis and Rudy Slater arrived and took seats in the front row. Murph Kelly was right behind them. The trainer glanced around the room. "All right, Coach," he said gruffly. "They're all here."

Mike Stone got up easily from his chair and moved to the center of the room. He held a blue marker in his hand and tossed it in the air and caught it several times before speaking. "Men," he said softly, "you know how I feel about the game you played Saturday night. You know, too, how I feel about a man looking over his shoulder. It's an utter waste of time. The Northern State game is history. Our big job now is to concentrate on the upcoming games.

"Everywhere I went today, on campus and around town, all I heard was talk of the national tournament. Everyone I met was up in arms because we've been left out in the cold. I suspect you've been subjected to the same kind of attention. Anyway, that's what I want to talk about before we get busy on the Southwestern scouting notes.

"First, our *big* objective is to win the conference

championship. After that, we can concentrate on national honors. Dad Young is working on the NCAA problem. Our problem is more important. We've got to keep winning.

"All of us, Dad Young, you, and I, would look foolish if we made a big ruckus about being overlooked and then got knocked off. Personally, I prefer to win games and let the victories do the talking."

The coach swiftly pivoted and walked back to his desk. Picking up a yardstick, he pointed it toward the board. "There's the Southwestern story. I've scouted SWU fifteen times in the past five years, twice before this year's Invitational Tournament at the Garden in New York. I know the SW players and what they can do, and that goes for Coach Jeff Habley and the type of strategy he's likely to use too.

"Starting at the left and extending across the top of the board you'll see the names of Southwestern's starting team. The important statistics are shown under each name, and our starting match-ups are shown at the bottom of the respective columns.

"Suppose we study Kinser's stats for a minute or so before discussing them."

Chip knew a lot about Kinser. The big forward was leading the country in scoring and had been on everybody's all-American team the previous year. He was a cinch to repeat this year. Chip glanced quickly at the bottom of the column. As he had figured, Stone had matched him against Kinser.

"All right," Stone began. He waited until he had their attention and then pointed the ruler at Kinser's column. "First, Kinser is the top scorer in the country. He's averaging around forty points a game. His shooting average is more than 45 percent. That means he makes nearly half of the shots he takes. He's the man we have to stop, and I'm counting on Chip to do it.

IN A MESS

"Now let's take a look at their overall team stats before we watch some tapes of their games."

SOUTHWESTERN UNIVERSITY

Starters	Kinser	Polk	Myer	Bordon	Lloyd
Numbers	14	23	55	54	33
Age	22	23	20	23	20
Height	6-6	6-3	6-3	6-11	6-7
Weight	195	200	175	240	200
Right (R)-Left (L)	R	L	R	R	R
Aggressiveness	E	E	E	E	E
Self-Control	P	P	F	F	G

Offensive Stats

	Kinser	Polk	Myer	Bordon	Lloyd
Scoring Avg.	40.3	21	9	12	5
Scoring %	.45	.30	.36	.50	.30
Speed	E	G	G	P	P
Leap	E	G	G	G	G
Hands	E	F	G	G	F
Footwork	E	F	G	P	F
Dribbling	E	E	G	P	F
Screening	P	E	G	E	F
Passing	F	P	G	G	F
Assists	P	P	E	G	F
Fumbles	No	No	Yes	No	Yes
Charging Fouls	Yes	No	Yes	No	Yes
Off. Rebounds	P	G	F	E	F
Off. Weakness	Needs Ball	Poor hands	Only right	Slow	Slow
Off. Team Play	P	G	F	G	F
Matchups	Hilton Freeman Hunter	Slater Tucker Smith	Chung Reardon Morris	Phillips Williams	Di Santis Hicks

"Kinser's twenty-two, stands six-six, and weighs 195 pounds. He's right-handed and very aggressive, but he has poor control of his emotions.

"Let's check his offensive stats now. His speed, leap, hands, footwork, and dribbling are excellent. On to his screening, passing, and assists. Here we find the weaknesses that keep him from being a truly strong all-around player. Take over from there, Chip. Give us a complete analysis of Kinser's type of play."

Chip looked the chart over carefully. "Well," he said thoughtfully, "Kinser has speed and all the skills and shots. He's fast and his shooting average means he's a dead shot."

"What about his team play?" Coach Stone interrupted.

"The fact that he's a poor screener," Chip continued, "could mean he waits for the ball. Since his assists are poor and his passing is only rated as fair, he probably tries to score every time he gets the ball.

"His shooting accuracy may account for the fact that he doesn't follow in very much. The 'yes' in the charging fouls column means he drives a lot."

"How can that help your play?" Stone asked.

"Well, I won't have to worry much about him passing and screening or using give-and-go plays. So when he gets the ball, I can play him tight. And since he doesn't follow in, I can forget about boxing him out and help Branch and Dom with the rebounding."

"That's right," Stone replied. "The rest of you check the information on the other starters according to your match-ups. Each of you should focus on your expected match-up."

Chip wrote the Kinser stats in his notebook and then added the items he and Coach Stone had discussed. That done, he shifted his attention to the other four starters. It was a big team with each player averaging more than two hundred pounds in weight, and plenty of height. Bordon was six-eleven, Lloyd six-seven, Kinser six-six, and the two backcourt men each six-three. It all spelled power.

SOUTHWESTERN UNIVERSITY

Starters	Kinser	Polk	Myer	Bordon	Lloyd
Numbers	14	23	55	54	33
Defensive Stats					
Personal Guarding	P	P	G	F	F
Speed	E	G	G	P	P
Hands	E	G	G	F	F
Footwork	E	G	G	P	F
Tight(T)-Loose(L)	L	L	T	T	T
Front-Slide-Switch	P	F	P	P	G
Interceptions	E	F	P	P	P
Will Foul	Y	Y	N	N	Y
Blocking-Out	N	N	Y	Y	Y
Rebounding	N	N	Y	Y	Y
Pressure	N	N	F	F	Y
Def. Weakness	Turns Head	Plays Ball	Over Aggressive	Slow	Slow
Def. Team Play	P	P	G	F	F

"Review their defensive stats now," Stone said. "Jimmy, suppose you take over."

Jimmy Chung quickly rose to his feet, but he didn't answer for a moment, which gave Chip a chance to study the speedster. At just under five-ten, Jimmy was the second smallest man on the squad. He was a dazzling dribbler and had a deadly jump shot. Jimmy was a wonderful playmaker, and his fast hands were perfect for the ball hawking at which he excelled.

"I don't think Southwestern plays very good defense," Jimmy said thoughtfully. "The personal guarding stats suggest that Kinser and Polk are poor and Bordon and Lloyd are only fair. Myer is really the only good defensive player they have."

"Right!" Stone said. "They get by mostly on power and control of the boards. What else, Jimmy?"

"Their use of the front, slide, and switch is poor."

"What does that mean?" Stone queried.

"It means our shuffle offense will work. If we keep moving and force them to do a lot of switching, we should be able to get some wide-open shots."

"That's the ticket," Mike Stone agreed. "And that's exactly what we're going to do Wednesday night. We'll use the shuffle and move the ball, and we'll keep it hopping. Take ten minutes to copy the stats, and then we'll go out on the floor and work on our defense. Tomorrow, we'll polish up the shuffle."

Ten minutes later, Coach Stone called time and led the team out on the court. Coach Hank Rockwell and the freshman team were sitting in the bleachers on the side of the court. Five of the freshmen wore Southwestern numbers. Stone quickly made the match-ups that had been written on the white board. Chip glanced over at Soapy. The redhead had been right about the size of the freshmen. They stood head and shoulders above the varsity, with the exception of Branch Phillips.

For the next two hours they worked against Southwestern's plays. At first the freshman players walked through them. Then the plays were stepped up until everyone was moving at full speed. It was a hard workout, and Chip was glad when Coach Stone called it a day. He and Soapy hustled down to the locker room, and fifteen minutes later they were on their way downtown to Grayson's.

IN A MESS

At the first newsstand they passed, Soapy paused long enough to feed the machine some quarters and buy a copy of the *Northern Times*. Chip kept right on going. He had gone less than fifty feet when he heard his pal coming up behind him on a dead run.

"Look at this!" Soapy cried, pointing to an article on the sports page. The redhead's demoralized tone of voice forewarned Chip, but he was far from prepared for the heading that leaped out of the paper. He stopped in his tracks and scanned the story in disbelief.

STATE BASKETBALL PLAYERS PROTEST NCAA ACTION
State Player Voices Threats Against Chair
by Sam Star

Interviewed Sunday morning after defeating Northern State University the previous night, State University players bitterly protested the NCAA Selection Committee's action in eliminating them from the national basketball tournament, better known as March Madness. One of the players went so far as to threaten Committee Chair Thomas Merrell with physical violence "if he ever saw him."

"Oh, no! Not now!" Chip exclaimed, glancing quickly at Soapy. "Now we *are* in a mess."

CHAPTER 7

Soapy's Secret Symbol

PEDESTRIANS PASSING Chip and Soapy on the street stared curiously at the two figures who looked as rigid as the Christmas ice sculptures still gracing University Park. Neither said a word. Neither had to. Soapy's eyes looked down at the icy sidewalk, and Chip stared with unseeing eyes at a sale sign in one of the department store windows. Both were deep in thought, completely unaware of their surroundings and the puzzled passersby streaming past them.

Soapy broke the silence. "Oh, no, Chip," he moaned. "I didn't *mean* that. Why did he print that? What'll we do?"

"I know what *you're* going to do," Chip said pointedly, directly meeting Soapy's eyes. "You're going to hike right back to Assembly Hall and catch Coach Stone before he goes home."

"But what will I tell him?"

"What else? Tell him the truth. Tell him before someone else beats you to it. You'll feel much better, but more than that, it's the right thing to do."

"I hope he hasn't seen the paper yet," Soapy muttered.

"He hasn't had a chance to see it, Soapy. It doesn't hit the stands until five o'clock. You can beat him to it." Chip extended the paper in his outstretched hand to Soapy. "Here!" he said sharply, "show it to him. Get going! We'll cover for you at the fountain."

Soapy turned and took off running without another word. Chip continued on down Main Street. On the way, he passed the University Savings and Loan Association offices and glanced in the large plate-glass window at the front. Although most businesses had closed for the day, the lights were still on in the front office, and Landon Davis, Cara's father, was engrossed in some papers. Even before they had met the man, Chip and Soapy had often seen him working late as they passed by the savings and loan company after practice on their way to the store.

Chip looked in the store windows along the way to Grayson's, which was located several blocks away. As soon as he entered the store, he sensed that Sam Star's blast had preceded him.

Mitzi quickly confirmed that thought. In her neatly manicured fingertips she held two papers out to him as he passed the cashier's desk. "Bad news, Chipper," she said sympathetically.

Chip took the papers, thanked her, and moved on through the store to the stockroom. The door was locked, and Chip breathed a sigh of relief. At least he would have a few quiet minutes to think things out. He let himself in and walked over to the desk. Unfolding the first newspaper Mitzi had given to him, the *Northern Times,* he glanced over Star's story again and then put the paper aside.

He picked up the *Herald* and turned to Bill Bell's column. The friendly writer had written the same sort of article as had Jim Locke. Chip shifted his attention back to Sam Star's story and read it carefully.

Afterward, he leaned back in the chair, trying to figure out just what could happen. One thing was certain: Sam Star's story could cause a lot of trouble for Soapy Smith if someone tried to make a big deal out of it. People who really knew Soapy understood that his belligerence was merely used to lighten tense or uncomfortable situations. In spite of himself and their situation, Chip had to smile. Soapy was a kind person and wouldn't threaten anyone!

A little later, Soapy arrived. One glance at his friend's woeful expression told the story all too clearly. Soapy was down, way down.

"What happened?" Chip asked.

"Coach was pretty hot."

"What did he say?"

"What didn't he say? He said I ought to learn when to talk and when to keep my big mouth shut."

"Then what?"

"Wasn't that enough? Well, he said for me to report to Dad Young's office first thing in the morning. I don't think Coach likes me very much."

"Nonsense. Of course he does, Soapy. Now stop worrying and get to work. I'll go along with you in the morning."

Monday evenings were usually slow at Grayson's, and this Monday was no exception. Although Chip knew that Skip and Lonnie were dying to talk basketball, he didn't give them a chance. Instead, he kept them on the move. He sent them home early and tried to do a little studying, but it was no use. He just couldn't concentrate.

Soapy came back to the stockroom at ten o'clock. The two friends struck out for Jefferson Hall with Chip setting a pace that gave the redhead little chance to talk.

Chip was tired. Perhaps discouraged was a better word, but he wasn't going to let Soapy know his true feelings. He quickly changed into his sweats, flossed and brushed his teeth, and hopped into bed.

Soapy was up early the next morning and brought back a copy of the *News*. But Chip was in no mood to read the paper. He substituted basketball instead and forced Soapy to join him in reviewing every move of the shuffle.

Opening the first photocopied sheet of the series, Chip spread it out on his desk. They checked the moves and options together. Coach Stone thought the shuffle would tie Southwestern in knots, and that was enough for Chip. Stone would make sure the Statesmen studied it until they could run the pattern blindfolded.

SPECIAL SHUFFLE OFFENSE FOR SWU

1. *All* players must follow the pattern.
2. The correct moves will draw Bordon, Lloyd, and Kinser out of rebound position and force them to move.
3. No shot is to be taken before at least seven passes; more are preferred.
4. Be aware of the time on the shot clock—Thirty-five seconds are a long time!

"If we keep moving like that and hold the ball," Soapy said tentatively, "Southwestern's gonna get good and mad."

"That's the general idea, Soapy," Chip said, nodding and smiling.

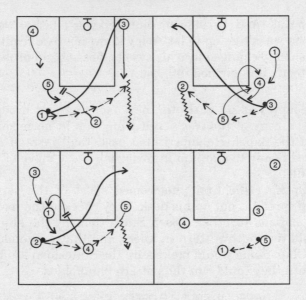

"You think Stone really means it? Do you think he really expects us to make all those passes before we take a shot?"

"That's right," Chip quietly affirmed.

"We'll be lucky to get out of there alive."

"The big thing is to win the game."

"Do or die, right?" Soapy ventured.

"Don't be funny," Chip said shortly.

They managed to review all the shuffle options and variations before it was time to start for Assembly Hall. Taking the usual shortcut through the park, they walked along beside University Stadium, home to State University football, until they came to the gym and athletic offices. Beyond the trophy lobby, they took the broad left ramp up one level and then walked along the hall past the basketball office to Dad Young's office. Dad Young and Mike Stone were waiting. The director of athletics got right to the point.

"Robert Smith," Young said softly, "Coach Stone tells me you are the player referred to in yesterday's paper, in the Sam Star article. Do you want to tell me about it?"

Soapy first shook his head, then nodded, and finally got the words out. "Yes, sir," he managed. "You see, it happened in the lobby of the hotel right after Mr. Star was talking to you. I was right behind him, and I was just talking out loud to myself. I do that a lot, sir." Soapy reddened and then continued. "I never meant my words to be taken as a threat against anyone, sir. I've never even met the man Mr. Star said I threatened."

"But you did mention Tom Merrell's name, didn't you? You *were* talking to Sam Star, isn't that true?"

"No, sir. I was walking behind him and I said that comment to no one in particular. He heard me and turned around and said he was going to print it. I thought he was kidding."

"Not him," Stone observed sourly.

"What about it, Chip?" Young asked. "Were you or any other players close enough to hear what was said?"

"Yes, sir, I was. Soapy certainly wasn't talking to Mr. Star, and he wasn't serious. He talks that way most of the time. We're all used to it."

Young turned back to Soapy. "You didn't say anything else about Mr. Merrell, did you?"

"No, sir. That is . . . well, no, sir."

There was something strange about Soapy's answer. Chip made a mental note to check it out as soon as they were alone.

After a short silence, Young got to his feet. "Well, Mike," he said, turning to the coach, "I suppose we've got to take *some* kind of action, but for the life of me, I don't know what. Do you have any ideas?"

Mike Stone frowned and shook his head. He ran a hand through his thick black hair. "No," he said, "I don't. It seems to me we've done about all that's necessary.

Don't get me wrong, Dad. I'm not sticking my neck out for Soapy Smith. Heaven forbid! He's always up to something, but I don't want to upset the team. Frankly, I'm in favor of letting it ride."

"All right," Young said heavily. "That's what we'll do." He paused to shake a finger under Soapy's nose. "As for you, Smith, you button up your lips and keep them that way. Can you remember that?"

"Yes, sir," Soapy said fervently.

"Remember something else," Coach Stone added. "You make just one more bad bounce, and you can turn in your uniform."

"Yes, sir," Soapy said meekly.

"All right," Young said, "you're both excused. Remember now, both of you, I don't want you talking about this matter to anyone." He looked at Chip and grunted. "You're in charge of this redheaded rascal, Hilton. Keep him away from newspaper reporters."

The two lifelong friends murmured their thanks and retraced their footsteps back down the hall, down the ramp, and out the large glass doors of Assembly Hall. On the way through the park, Chip remembered how Soapy had sputtered when Young referred to the chairman of the selection committee. "All right," he said, "out with it! What's the rest of the Merrell business?"

"Well," Soapy said reluctantly, "I sent a few telegrams, lots of regular letters, some E-mails, and even some overnight FedEx letters—some to Mr. Merrell and some to the other members of the committee. Then I sent some to Mr. King, the conference commissioner, and a few to the presidents of A & M and Northern State." Soapy paused and added quickly, "I didn't sign them though. That is, except for my secret symbol."

Chip sighed, amazed once again by his pal. "Do you need any help?" he asked.

"Nah, this one's all me," Soapy said quietly. "I needed more postage money, but Mr. Grayson gave me an advance, so it's OK."

"Just don't write anything controversial," Chip warned. "The last thing we need is to have more of that."

"I'm being careful," Soapy replied. "But don't worry! They'll never find my secret symbol."

CHAPTER 8

The "SWU" Treatment

THE PLANE droned steadily through the sky with scarcely a quiver, and it was hard to believe that the big silver bird was speeding along at better than three hundred and fifty miles an hour. Chip watched the cottony clouds slide past the window for a moment and then leaned back in his seat and closed his eyes.

He tried to force the Southwestern University game out of his thoughts by recalling yesterday's events: the excitement that had gripped the student body and fans, the final practice, and, last night, the big campus sports rally.

Soapy had bought every out-of-town newspaper available at the airport gift shops and read every line of the sports pages. Even now, the redhead was at the back of the plane checking out the plane's newspapers. So far there had been no word from the selection committee, no indication that it was even considering a change in the decision.

Now, with their destination of Hawthorne only minutes away, details of the Statesmen's last visit to Southwestern came vividly to Chip's mind. He smiled wryly as he thought of the "treatment" that all visiting teams had to face when they invaded the SW hoop roost. He and his teammates had been given the works the last time. They hadn't been ready for it then, but now they knew what to expect.

A flight attendant passed by and gently touched him on the shoulder. "Fasten your seat belt, please," she said.

Chip sat up and was fastening the seat belt when Soapy reappeared. The redhead threw himself down in his seat and ran his hands roughly through his hair. "No luck, Chip," he said dejectedly. "I don't get it! One of those big-shot writers ought to have something to say about the selection committee."

Chip wasn't going to be drawn into that discussion again. He nodded and turned to look out the window. The airport was directly below. The plane circled to the left, dipping a wing on his side. Now he had a full view of the long runways and the terminal. The pilot completed the turn and leveled off, and the plane descended swiftly and gently with the wheels touching down on the runway as smoothly as one of Jimmy Chung's layups against a glass backboard. Turning at the end of the runway, the plane taxied swiftly back toward the terminal and parked in front of the main building.

As soon as the pilot shut down the engines, the Statesmen were on their feet, eager to finish this part of the journey and get on with their preparations for the game.

With Soapy right behind him, Andre Gilbert led the way to the exit door where the flight attendants were standing and on up the ramp into the terminal. Chip followed, looking at the waiting crowd gathered beyond the gate, but it was Soapy who first saw the signs. "Look, Chip!" he cried. "There must be a strike. They're picketing the plane."

"Not quite," said one of the passengers pointedly. "They're waiting for some of the passengers. Guess who?"

"You must be a Southwestern fan. Looks like they're giving us the friendly traditional big welcome, eh?" Soapy retorted, swaggering into the gate area.

It was quite a reception. There were about fifty Southwestern students in the crowd, and many were carrying orange and white posters. They made a long lane through which the Statesmen were forced to pass on their way to the terminal lobby and baggage claim area. And, although it was intended to be fun, some of the jibes showed little respect for sportsmanship.

"Here come the cry babies!"

"No, not cry babies. Why, they're fighters. They're gonna beat up the old men on the NCAA committee."

"You mean they're mad about the national tournament?"

"Sure! They talk a good game too!"

"Which one is Hilton? I wanna get a picture of him before he runs up against our man Kinser."

"They don't look like much."

"Maybe not, but what a record!"

"Aw, it isn't so bad. They've only lost *eight* games."

"Nine, counting tonight."

This volley brought a big laugh from the crowd, but it failed to ruffle the composure of most of the Statesmen. They smiled and plowed steadily ahead, ignoring the taunts. But not Soapy! This was his kind of crowd! He was a master of repartee and he fenced with the hecklers all the way through the building, at the baggage carousel, and out to the bus.

The players grabbed their team traveling bags off the carousel, passed through the doors, and swung their gear into the open underbelly of the bus. Coach Mike Stone was the last to climb aboard the bus before they were off.

The trip was peaceful enough until they started through the city near the campus. Then ten or twelve cars decorated with the SW colors of orange and white caught up with the bus. Some of the cars cut in front of the bus while the others fell in behind. Then, as if given a signal, the drivers began blaring their horns. Whether by design or not, the bus driver immediately slowed down until the bus was barely crawling.

People began to pour out of the stores and line the sidewalks, shouting and waving pennants, and the occupants of cars parked along the street began to blast their horns.

"Hey, guys, look at the signs in the windows. Chip, they've posted your game number in the windows," Soapy yelled.

"Soapy, I think they have something else in mind," Chip said, laughing.

Number 44 was painted on every window, sometimes in white and sometimes in orange. Short, punchy phrases were painted on many of the windows.

WELCOME VICTIMS

NUMBER 44 TONIGHT

REVENGE IS SWEET

THE END OF A PERFECT SEASON

NCAA—THEY SELECT ONLY THE BEST—SW

Coach Mike Stone stood quietly in the aisle in the front of the bus. His jaw was set and his gaze was angry, but he said nothing. The bus crawled along and eventually reached the end of the business section. A little farther on it turned in at the Southwestern campus entrance.

Chip remembered Southwestern's campus hotel, the Southwestern Inn. It was one of the best university conference hotels in the country and equipped with every modern convenience. As a part of the school's hotel management course, it was operated almost exclusively by student personnel.

The bus had scarcely pulled to a stop in front of the hotel when the treatment crowd again appeared with signs and taunts. The SW fans formed a lane through the doors to the hotel lobby, and, once again, Chip and Soapy and the rest of the team had to run the gauntlet.

Soapy was the target of most of the jibes, and he loved every minute of it, but this time he could do nothing about it. Coach Stone stood beside the lane and kept his eyes on Soapy. He waited until everyone had passed through before following the players into the hotel. Chip noted there were no signs and no noisy fans inside the lobby. That hadn't been true the last time. Evidently some progress was being made in the spirit of hospitality.

The bellhops carried the luggage into the lobby and placed the bags near the elevator as Andre Gilbert passed out the room keys.

As usual, Chip and Soapy were roommates. They searched out their bags, took the elevator, and were soon in their room. Soapy had picked up the Southwestern papers and didn't even take time to unpack. He flopped down on his bed and began to check the sports pages. Chip emptied his bag and hung up his clothes. Then he lay down on his bed and let his thoughts speed ahead to the game. The coming battle meant either the beginning or the end of State's struggle for recognition.

THE "SWU" TREATMENT

There wasn't an empty seat in sight in the huge Southwestern University Arena. It seemed to Chip that every person in the field house was yelling at the top of his lungs. The "sold out" sign had been posted at all the entrances to the arena. Fans spilled out into the aisles and stood three deep around the court as the pregame festivities commenced. Restlessness, excitement, and tension crackled in the air.

On cue, the Southwestern players were the first to appear on the court. The crowd responded with frenzied shouts, cheers, and whistles every time one of the white-clad stars dropped a ball down through the net.

As a preview of their upcoming game treatment, the Statesmen emerged to loud booing from every nook and cranny of the arena as they took to their end of the court. With little notice from the SWU fans, the Statesmen worked on their passing drills, sharpening up their timing and getting the feel of the floor.

Chip cast a wary eye toward the SWU players from time to time. Coach Stone had instructed him to make sure he and his teammates weren't left behind when the home team left the court.

"They like to slip off the floor and leave their opponents to get caught in the pitch-dark arena when the lights go off," Stone had warned. "It's all a part of their so-called *sportsmanlike* treatment."

Chip remembered his feelings the previous year. He recalled his embarrassment and anger when sheer blackness had occurred while he was in the act of catching a ball. He had ended up with a jammed finger on his shooting hand. That wasn't going to happen tonight.

He flipped a high, loop pass to Branch, a pass the big player pulled in deftly and surely with one hand. Changing direction, Chip cut down the lane at full speed. Branch faked beautifully and then made a perfect backhand bounce pass to Jimmy, who was cutting under the basket from the other side of the court. Chip grinned. A year ago, Branch couldn't have caught the ball with a big fishing net. Now he was a skilled basketball player and had helped to make the team the success it was today.

Chip trotted back up the side of the court in time to see Kinser, Bordon, Lloyd, Myer, and Polk walk off the court in the direction of the home-team player aisle. He called for the ball and immediately rolled it off the court to Andre Gilbert. Then he walked to the sideline and stood beside Coach Stone. Without a word, each of his teammates quickly and quietly followed Chip's actions.

Suddenly, without warning, the arena darkened. The only lights remaining were those above the exits, and they were dim and far away. The great crowd quieted. Then the darkness was broken by five shafts of light, each one focused on one of five giant hoops standing along the baseline under the Southwestern basket. Each hoop was covered with orange crepe paper and a huge white painted "44" on the center.

Then, with a crashing of cymbals, the five SWU starters, dressed in their orange and white satin warmup suits, broke through the hoops. A spotlight followed each player one at a time, as he dribbled toward the other end of the court. The growing noise of the crowd was deafening.

The five stars reached the basket one at a time, with each leaping high above the rim and deftly dropping the ball into the net. Bordon, the big center, was first, followed by Lloyd, Kinser, Polk, and Myer. The lights came on, and after retrieving the practice balls, they ran back to the home bench, passing directly in front of the Statesmen.

"You're next!" "Dunk" Lloyd growled as he passed.

"Now you get the *real* SWU treatment," Kinser rasped.

The three officials moved to the center circle, and Kinser, the Southwestern captain, trotted out on the court. Stone nodded to Chip, and he walked out to represent State. "I guess you two players know each other," the referee said.

Kinser nodded, and Chip extended his hand. His big opponent tried a bone-crushing grip, but it didn't work. Chip had anticipated it and gave back as good as he received.

"Any questions?" the official asked.

Chip shook his head. The court was regulation size and the glass backboards, lines, and lighting were perfect.

"All right then," the referee said, "that's it." He gave a short blast on his whistle, and Chip walked back to the State University bench. He joined Coach Stone, Phillips, Chung, Di Santis, and Slater in the traditional team clasp. They waited for the Southwestern players to take the court.

As the SWU players took their positions on the court, the fans rose en masse and cheered them every step of the way. The Statesmen waited for the cheers to die down and then walked out to pair up with their rivals. Di Santis lined up against Lloyd, Chip walked to a position between Kinser and the SWU basket, and Jimmy Chung and Rudy Slater took the forward positions opposite the SWU guards Polk and Myer. Branch Phillips stopped opposite Bordon, just outside the restraining circle, and waited for the tap signal.

Chip gave the deep back-tap sign to Jimmy, and the speedster flashed it to Branch. As soon as he got the signal, Branch stepped into the jump circle and crouched for the game-opening jump ball.

The referee tossed the ball high and straight, and Branch went up like a kangaroo. His hand was a foot above Bordon's when he slapped the ball far back toward the SWU basket. It was a perfect back tap. Chip and Di Santis screened Kinser and Lloyd away from the ball, and Jimmy sped back from his forward position and gathered it in.

Without even breaking his stride, Jimmy reversed direction and dribbled hard for the State basket. Polk had followed Jimmy across the ten-second line, but he was unable to reverse fast enough to catch up, and Jimmy was all alone. There was plenty of daylight between Jimmy and the basket, but team play and respect for the coach came first with him. Coach Stone had said the first time they got the ball they were to pass it at least seven times before anyone took a shot.

As soon as the Statesmen were in shuffle formation, Jimmy passed the ball to Chip and made the first move. Chip passed to Di Santis coming up from the baseline on the weak side of the court and set a double screen beside Branch. Slater cut around the double screen, and Di Santis zipped the ball to him.

Slater had a wide-open shot near the free-throw line, and for a second, Chip thought Rudy had forgotten the strategy. Then Slater passed to Branch and cut, and the shuffle shifted to the other side of the court.

The fans didn't like it. They began to boo, stomp their feet, and shout out their fury and frustration. The hysteria had no effect on the Statesmen. They had anticipated this reaction. In fact, it was all part of their planned strategy.

The passing and shifting of the shuffle from one side of the court to the other continued, and now the SWU players began to show their irritation. They wanted the ball. They wanted to run up the score on their new victims and run the SU players off the court, off the campus, and out of their town. Chip and his teammates clearly recognized the tension that was building up in their opponents, and it strengthened their determination to stick with the team strategy.

Kinser was the first opponent to break. "What's the matter, Hilton?" he taunted. "Are you afraid to take a shot? Afraid to risk your scoring record against mine?"

Chip smiled but made no reply. He liked Stone's philosophy. Actions spoke louder than words!

Right after the seventh pass, Chip caught Kinser out of position and cut for the basket. He was wide open and directly in front of the hoop when Branch hit him with a hook pass. Without thinking, he leaped high in the air and dunked the ball, flipping it with all his might down through the ring and net for the first two points of the game just as the shot clock struck 00.

Chip was on his way down from the leap when Kinser crashed into him and sent him sprawling. The force of Kinser's charge carried them both out-of-bounds. They wound up face to face on the floor in a tangle of arms and legs.

"Laugh that one off, victim 44!" Kinser snarled, scrambling to his feet.

CHAPTER 9

Worthy of Victory

THE REFEREE was blasting his whistle and holding a closed fist above his head, indicating a foul on number 14—Kinser—when Chip got back on his feet. He had been hit hard and was still shaken up, but then he heard the abuse being directed toward the official by the crowd. Chip walked slowly to the free-throw line. It had been a deliberate foul, and the penalty could be two shots.

The official held the ball and waited for the crowd to quiet. When the noise continued, he raised his hand for silence, but this action seemed to incite the fans even more. The noise intensified.

Chip stepped back from the line and watched Kinser. The SWU captain had moved to his position in the lane, but he was protesting the call and motioning with his hands in an obvious attempt to attract attention.

The crowd noise gradually died away until, at last, the referee handed the ball to Chip. "One shot," he said.

Keeping his eyes focused on the ring and visualizing the shot, Chip bounced the ball four times. Then he arched the ball up and out, and it snapped the cords of the net as it passed through the basket.

Bordon took the ball out-of-bounds for SWU. Chip backpedaled into his defensive position, glancing up at the game clock and the shot clock on the way. If only he and the team could keep it up!

The SWU players came confidently and eagerly down the floor and set up in their two-three formation. Bordon was on the right side of the lane, close to the basket, and Lloyd and Kinser were in the corners. Polk and Myer took charge of the backcourt. The scouting notes had stressed that SWU's front line, Bordon, Kinser, and Lloyd, did most of the scoring. The "big three" did the shooting and followed all shots, made or missed.

Myer passed to Lloyd in the corner. The big forward fired a high pass to Bordon. The tall center faked left, turned right, and tried to shoot, but then Bordon got a surprise. Branch's big hand went right over the ball! He practically knocked it down Bordon's throat, which had never happened before. The move caught Bordon completely by surprise. He attempted to regain the ball, but it went spinning out of his reach. Branch swooped down and caught up the ball.

Chip had blocked Kinser away from the basket as soon as Bordon maneuvered for his shot. Now, with Branch in possession of the ball, he broke for the State University basket. Branch hit him with the ball, and Chip dribbled all alone along the right sideline.

Kinser was left far behind, and Chip could have gone all the way, but, like Jimmy, he slowed down and waited for his teammates. Then the Statesmen began the shuffle all over again. They worked the ball around, using as much of the shot clock as possible. Following Coach

Stone's game plan to pass the ball at least seven times before attempting a shot, they continued that effort until Bordon got tangled up in a switching situation.

Branch cut for the basket, and Chip hit him with a high, hard pass. Branch, almost moving in slow motion, laid the ball softly and surely against the backboard. State led 5-0.

The home team came down in a hurry the next time, determined to break into the scoring column. Polk passed the ball to Kinser on the left side of the court, and the scoring star scarcely looked at the basket before he let the ball fly for a long three-point attempt as if it were red hot. It was a bad shot and banged high against the backboard. Kinser tried to follow in but found Chip had him neatly boxed. Di Santis had screened Lloyd away from the hoop, and Branch was still guarding Bordon, playing him head-on, face-to-face, making no attempt to get the ball.

Jimmy Chung and Rudy Slater flew swiftly back from their frontcourt positions and made the rebound recovery. It was a new defensive technique as far as SWU was concerned. The Southwesterners retreated sullenly, shaking their heads as their frustration mounted.

State University advanced to the frontcourt and again began a slow, methodical, yet tantalizing shuffle attack. That was the pattern of the game for the first half. State's mixed-up offense had Southwestern bewildered, and the fact that the Statesmen wouldn't take a shot unless the man with the ball was wide open drained all the starch out of the SWU defense.

Offensively, Southwestern's power and "pound the board" attack never got started. State's blocking-out techniques and the collapsing action of the defensive front line stopped the "big three" cold.

The score at the half: State 37, Southwestern 22.

Mike Stone had the State reserves cleared from the bench and on their way to the visiting locker room before the half ended. And he was waiting at the visiting team's aisle for his five starters when the buzzer sounded. He led them swiftly through the aisle and along the hall to their locker room. Andre Gilbert was at the door and closed it as soon as the last player entered.

Murph Kelly had the sliced oranges and Gatorade drinks ready for Gilbert's complement of student managers to pass them out. Kelly moved from player to player passing out new towels. Coach Stone stood just inside the door checking some notes he had made during the first half.

"Relax," Kelly barked. "All of you! Stretch your feet out to full length and lean back against the wall."

Not another word was spoken for a full five minutes. Soapy tried to talk to Chip with sign language, holding his hands on the side away from Stone and awkwardly forming the letters, but Chip couldn't make them out and shook his head.

Soapy tried once more. Chip still couldn't understand what the redhead was saying, so Soapy groaned and sat on his hands. Just a minute or so later, Stone strode to the center of the room. Everyone sat up and paid attention.

"Great job, men!" he said vibrantly. "Just great! Everything is going according to plan." He stopped and took a turn across the room and back.

"This game is far from over though," he continued in a warning voice. "I know Coach Habley all too well. That old fox is cooking up something different right now and reading each player the riot act. He'll work them into a feverish pitch. Be ready for more aggressiveness by each player.

"I'm sure he'll have all five of them crashing the offensive board every time they take a shot. That will give them a chance to get the ball back. After all, that's their game.

"So we're going to cross them up. We're going to leave it to Branch and Di Santis and Chip to get the rebounds. Jimmy, you and Rudy tear out of there and break for our basket every time their backcourt men crash the boards. Got it?"

Mike Stone looked at each of the five starters and smiled briefly when they nodded in agreement. "Chip," he added, "I want you to take a chance and break every time the ball comes off the board on the side away from you. Understand?"

Chip nodded and Stone continued. "One other thing: If they don't crash the boards, forget the fast break and stick with your possession game. Remember, they like to score. If they don't have the ball, they lose their poise."

Chip sensed that their coach was laboring under a terrific emotional strain. It wasn't easy to sit on the bench and let nothing interfere with a cold analysis of the game. Only the greatest coaches had the ability to do that. He guessed that was the reason some mentors were more successful than others.

Stone's voice broke through Chip's thoughts. "Oh, I nearly forgot," Stone said. "They will undoubtedly change their defense. I wouldn't be surprised to see Habley send them into a zone. If he does, we'll fire from the outside with Chip doing most of the shooting. Branch, you and Dom and Rudy will have to follow in the shots. Maybe a few State three-pointers will give them a dose of their own medicine."

Stone paused and then extended his hand for the team clasp. "Let's go, guys," he said softly.

Murph Kelly, Andre Gilbert, and every player in the room crowded into the circle that surrounded Stone. It was the first team clasp Chip could remember in which no words were spoken, no challenging yells uttered—

none were needed. There was absolute silence as their hands, one upon the other, met and held. Chip felt sure every person in that circle was, like him, breathing a sort of prayer—a prayer that their team would be worthy of victory.

CHAPTER 10

A Place
in the Sun

SOMEONE BANGED on the door and yelled "Time," breaking the spell. There was a mad scramble as the teammates lined up to follow their captain, William "Chip" Hilton, out on the court.

The home team players had evidently been out on the floor for some time, because they were shooting at both ends of the court. The five SWU starters were shooting at their second-half basket, and the rest of the squad stood at State's second-half basket. These players delayed leaving as long as possible, but it wasn't a surprise, just more of the SWU special treatment. The Statesmen didn't really need these few shots, however. They had been ready for this game for a long time.

Chip got in only one practice shot before the buzzer sounded and the three officials walked to their floor positions to start the second half. Four SWU players stalked out on the floor as one waited impatiently at midcourt for the official to hand him the ball for the second-half throw-in. Waiting in their positions, the SWU players sullenly sized up their respective rivals as the Statesmen moved to opposite stations.

There was no effort on the part of the players of either team to shake hands. That courtesy was the responsibility of the home team, and the SWU players hadn't even extended it at the start of the game. The lineups for the second half were the same as at the start of the game. There had been only a few substitutions so far in this game, and there weren't likely to be many more. Both coaches had started their best and stuck with them.

The second half began on a sour note for Southwestern. Chip quickly gobbled up Polk's lazy inbound pass to Myer and immediately flipped the ball over to Di Santis. Di Santis took charge of the prized ball and returned a sharp bounce pass to Chip, who was moving up from his inbound position. Chip dribbled across the ten-second line and over to the right side of the court. His teammates quickly took their shuffle positions before Chip passed to Jimmy and cut past Branch to start their offensive attack.

He knew something was wrong as soon as he made the first stride. Kinser made no attempt to stick with him, instead switching to cover Slater, while Polk picked Chip up as he cut through the lane. Habley had changed the SWU defense to permit an automatic switch every time the Statesmen crossed or screened. Coach Stone had called the turn by the old fox after all.

Chip immediately reversed, and Jimmy passed the ball back to him. Branch broke to a high-post position in the outer half of the free-throw circle. Chip bounced the ball in to State's big man, changed direction, and cut down the middle.

Branch faked and turned away as Chip cut through. Then he returned a bounce pass, which caught Chip waist high as he cut across the lane. Chip gathered in the ball, threw a hard stop, and went up for a short jumper. The ball spun neatly through the ring and took a little ride in the net before dropping on through for the score. The SWU crowd was silent.

Thanks to Stone's warning, Chip and his teammates had been ready. He slapped Branch on the back as they retreated to their defensive positions. The big guy had been the key in meeting the switching defense so quickly. That play would give Jeff Habley and his players something to think about.

Habley hadn't changed his team's offensive formation. The players lined up in their regular two-three formation and followed their usual formula. Myer passed to Kinser and then the scoring star passed over Chip's head to Bordon. This time Bordon faked a shot and then dribbled across the lane to the other side of the court.

Lloyd cut around the pivot-block and took the hand-off for the shot, but Branch switched on the pass and extended his long arms over Lloyd's head. The big corner man was forced to change the angle of his shot. The ball went too high, smacked off the ring, and bounced up in the air.

Chip boxed Kinser away from the lane and watched to see what would happen. Just as Stone had predicted, Polk and Myer came charging in for the offensive rebound. Chip held his position for a moment more. Then he saw Di Santis go up over Lloyd and hook the rebound out of the air. There was nothing to wait for now! Chip took off for the State basket. He was a stride past the ten-second line when Di Santis's swift peg whipped the ball into his hands.

There was daylight between him and the basket, and he hard dribbled straight for the hoop. Again, he couldn't resist the urge to dunk the ball. Chip leaped up and slammed the ball down through the basket with all his strength. He had always felt the dunk was a show-off play, but the Statesmen had taken enough from this bunch and had eaten enough crow to last them as long as they played basketball. He backtracked past the bench and gave Coach Stone a sharp salute. It was a flippant gesture and he knew it, but that was the way he felt. Their coach had outguessed Jeff Habley at every turn.

The rest of the game was a nightmarish blur for SWU. The fans never sat down, and they never stopped yelling. Coach Habley pulled all the stops, trying every trick he had accumulated in all his years of coaching. Defensively, he tried the man-to-man and the zone presses, half-court and full-court, two or three types of zones, the switching man-to-man, and finally a box-and-one.

In the box-and-one, he assigned Polk the job of sticking with Chip while the other four players formed a box formation in front of the basket. But nothing stopped Chip and nothing stopped the State offense!

Defensively, it was different for State University. The home team's power offense began to wear the Statesmen down. The home forces closed the gap to four points. Both teams were fighting desperately now, matching basket for basket.

With a minute and a half left to play, State still led by four points. Then, with Southwestern in possession, Polk's teammates set him up all alone on one side of the court for a one-on-one play. Slater was two inches taller than Polk but not quite as fast. He had successfully dogged the SWU playmaker all through the game, but now a tired Rudy fell for a head-and-shoulder fake. Polk cut around him and drove for the basket. Slater recovered but not quite quickly enough. He fouled Polk just as the playmaker released the ball for the shot. The ball skipped through the hoop as the referee blew his whistle for a foul.

Chip looked at the clock. Thirty seconds to play! The shot clock was no longer a factor. Polk made the free throw, and when Chip took the ball out-of-bounds, the scoreboard said it all: State 61, Southwestern 60. The three-point play had been disastrous.

SWU was pressing, and Chip wanted Jimmy to have the ball. The little ball handler was the greatest dribbler in the game. Chip raised the ball as a signal, and Jimmy broke to him with lightning speed. Chip bounced the ball inbounds to the dribbling wizard and sprinted up the sideline. In the frontcourt, he turned to watch Jimmy.

The little guy had never been better. He turned, twisted, and changed direction, and all the time his fingertips controlled the ball perfectly. Jimmy crossed the ten-second line and continued his dribbling.

Defensively, Myer closed in, his long arms extending to each side of Jimmy. Chip sensed now that Jimmy was afraid to pass, afraid to risk an interception. Chip risked a glance at the clock. Only ten seconds!

Then it happened!

Before Chip could grasp that the ball had been intercepted, that Jimmy had passed to him just as he turned to look at the clock, Kinser was dribbling at full speed toward the Southwestern goal. Chip took after the speeding dribbler, his heart pounding heavily. But even as he started, he realized he could never catch Kinser. An agonizing cry burst from his lips. He had lost the game!

Then he saw Branch tearing up the opposite sideline, his long legs fairly eating up the distance. Chip tried to gauge the distance between Branch and Kinser. Even as he watched, he saw that the big center was gaining. By now Kinser was at the free-throw line. After another stride he went up in the air for the shot.

Branch was still behind Kinser, but he took off in a flying leap like a startled bird, heading straight for the basket, one long arm straining at full length. His finger-tips barely reached the ball as it kissed the backboard on its upward flight. It was contact enough, however! The deflected ball was knocked off the line and back into Chip's hands.

As he turned to dribble upcourt, the buzzer ended the game. Chip threw the ball high in the air, high above the basket. Underdog State University had won the impossible game, scored a one-point victory, upset the champions on their own court, and earned a place in the sun!

Then Chip remembered Branch Phillips. The big player had crashed far behind the basket and rammed headlong into the crowd. Chip turned eagerly to look, and then he saw the crowd looking down at the aisle between the rows of seats behind the basket. Branch wasn't getting up!

CHAPTER 11

Sanity and Fair Play Prevail

MURPH KELLY and Mike Stone passed Chip on the dead run. They pushed their way through the fans, and Chip followed. As Murph checked the injury, Chip knelt beside Branch and lifted his head.

"I'm all right, Chip," Branch reassured him. "It's just my back. I can't straighten up." He tried to rise, but Kelly pushed him back.

"I'll get the collapsible stretcher," Stone said. "Stay with him, Chip."

The rest of the State players were crowding forward, but Coach Stone motioned them away. "Andre!" he barked. "Have the assistant coaches take the team down to the locker room. Players, get showered and dressed. Andre, keep them there until you hear from me. We'll take care of Phillips. Get going now."

Soapy tossed Chip's warm-up jacket to him and reluctantly followed his teammates. The sideline crowd had spilled out on the court and was trying to push forward to see Phillips. The arena ushers and security arrived then and gradually cleared the court. Chip looked curiously around the vast gym. The fans weren't yelling now. They were instead filing quietly out of the mezzanine, balcony, and court-level seats, all appearing subdued and disappointed. Coach Jeff Habley and his players had already disappeared.

Chip talked to Branch about the game, but his thoughts were all tied up in knots. The team had reached the heights at last and now, with one little mishap, was right back where it had been all season. He tried to put the A & M and Northern State University games out of his thoughts, but it was no use. What if Branch couldn't play in the A & M game? Or in the Northern State game? Or in both of them? What if he was out for the rest of the season? Or out of basketball for good?

Stone came back with the SWU trainer and a stretcher, and, despite Branch's protests, they lifted him on the stretcher and rolled him across the court and along the main corridor of the building to a back exit. An ambulance backed up to the platform just as they arrived.

"The school hospital is only a block away," the SWU trainer briefly explained. "We can have an X ray in half an hour."

"I'll go along," Chip offered.

"You will not!" Kelly commanded. "Get back to the locker room and get dressed. Tell Gilbert to stay there until I get back."

"Everything is set for the team to eat at the hotel," Stone added. "The assistant coaches will take you guys over there and get started. I'll be there soon. Another thing, no one leaves the dining room until I get there."

Chip nodded and moved over beside Branch. He ruffled the big player's hair fondly. "You won the game for us," Chip said in admiration. "It was the greatest save I ever saw."

"You can say that again!" Stone muttered, hoping to cheer up his fallen player. "It might even make the Play of the Day. Chip, you need to get going. Take charge of the team."

Chip heard his teammates before he reached the locker room. They hadn't forgotten Branch, but the victory had overwhelmed them. It dawned on Chip that State University was suddenly a somebody on the national scene. He pounded on the door, and when Andre Gilbert opened it a crack, he heard Soapy yell: "Go away! Men at play!"

Andre pulled the door open wide and yanked him into the room. The guys saw him and gave him a going-over, ending the pummeling by lifting him up on the trainers' table and demanding a speech. Chip didn't want to break up the celebration, but he did want to talk about Branch. He told them what had happened and said they would get a complete report at the hotel later on. When he told them Coach Stone had said they were to go with the assistant coaches to the hotel to have dinner, the celebration broke up, and they began piling into their clothes.

"Let's go!" Soapy shouted. "We gotta find out how A & M and Northern State made out."

The team finished dressing quickly and headed for the campus hotel. Andre Gilbert remained behind, packing all the equipment into the traveling trunk. The manager of the hotel restaurant was waiting and seated them at a long table in the center of the banquet room. "You boys sure upset the SWU apple cart for the second time," he said pleasantly. "You must have their number. Anyway, congratulations. Which one of you is Hilton?"

Soapy had taken a spot beside Chip and raised a hand over his head to point out his friend. "That's him," he said. "Why?"

The man sized Chip up and shook his head in admiration. "Oh, I just wanted to see the player who could tie Kinser in knots, that's all. We heard the game on the radio, and about all the announcer was talking about was the duel between the two of them."

The man addressed Chip. "The announcer said you got forty-two points. Is that right?"

"I don't know," Chip said quietly.

"That's right," Soapy said quickly. "Kinser only got seventeen. Why, if Chip wanted to be a, well, a shooter like Kinser, he could average fifty or sixty points a game."

The man grinned. "You started to say 'ball hog,' didn't you?"

Soapy nodded politely. "Yes, I did. Especially since you brought it up."

"That's been mentioned a lot of times around here," the man said sourly. "Some of us think that team needs four or five basketballs on offense. And most of us are glad Kinser got some of the arrogance knocked out of him."

"When can we get the scores of the other games?" Soapy asked.

"At eleven o'clock," their host said. He glanced at his watch. "That gives you plenty of time for your dinner. There are no TVs in the dining room or lobby, so you'll have to watch the sports news in your rooms. I guess I'd better get some more food out here. It looks like a few of you don't miss many meals."

Everyone laughed and agreed when Soapy spoke up: "Hey, I resemble that last remark!"

The Statesmen began to talk, reliving the game. Chip seized the opportunity to ask Soapy what the finger talk in the locker room at the half had been all about.

"You need some practice," Chip said teasingly. "I didn't get it."

"Everything worked out all right," Soapy said smugly. "Anyway, I was trying to tell you to shoot more. Kinser couldn't even guard *me!* He turned his head on every pass and *never* boxed out. You can take the scoring championship away from him easily if you keep going."

Soapy pulled a piece of paper out of his pocket. "I've got the stats right here. Let's see. SWU finished up the regular season tonight with our game. Kinser has played in twenty-two games and scored 847 points for a 38.5 point average per game." He turned the paper over. "You've played in nineteen games and scored 708 points for an average of 37.2 points per game.

"That means he has only about 1.3 points more per game. Man! You can make that up in the next three games."

"There are only two left."

"Wrong! Old-timer, you forget the tournament."

"I'm not interested in points. I want State to win the conference."

"So does everybody else," Soapy retorted, "and we're going to do it! But a lot of us, including Coach Stone, want you to win the national scoring title. Kinser isn't a very popular guy!"

The next round of food arrived, and Soapy got busy again. Soon he and Speed were engaged in one of their entertaining arguments. "That's right," Soapy said loudly, making sure everyone heard him. "I met Kinser right after the game, and there was only one thing that kept me from tearing him apart."

"*You!*" Speed managed incredulously. "Tear *Kinser* apart!"

"That's right," Soapy repeated. "Only *one* thing."

"What was that?"

"*Fear!* Absolute fear!" Soapy yelped, laughing. "Just plain, ordinary fear."

The whole team began to needle Speed, and the barbs were really flying when Coach Stone, Murph Kelly, and Andre Gilbert arrived. That broke up the chatter, and the food was forgotten as the players waited for Kelly's report on Branch Phillips.

"It's a muscle spasm between the kidney and the hip," Kelly explained. "The X ray showed nothing."

"Is it serious?" Chip asked anxiously. "Will he be able to play Friday night?"

Kelly shrugged his shoulders. "That is anybody's guess, Hilton. Right now he can't move."

"Won't heat or some kind of therapy help?" someone asked.

"Yes, but we don't know how much," Kelly said slowly.

"He'll be able to go with us tomorrow morning," Coach Stone explained. "Whether or not Branch will be able to play Friday night is another question. You can be sure Murph is going to do everything in the book to get Branch ready. Murph will stay with him tonight at the hospital as a precaution."

The coach rubbed his hands together briskly and looked around at the players. "I didn't get a chance to tell you what a great game you played. You were great! All the way. Every way."

He paused and continued significantly, "Now let's put this food away and get to bed. The news comes on at eleven o'clock. I want the lights out right after the scores."

That brought a laugh before the players got back to the business of eating. Later they began to drift away and head for their rooms. When Chip and Soapy reached their room, Soapy sat down at the desk and began to write furiously. Chip turned on ESPN and listened for the collegiate scores.

When the collegiate sports segment came on, Soapy stopped writing long enough to hear the scores.

Northern State University had beaten A & M, 92-87. They knew already, of course, that State had upset Southwestern on the champions' home court by one point, 61-60. The redhead resumed his scribbling, completely disregarding the other scores. He came to attention, however, when the reporter talked about the big sports story of the day.

"The big sports story of the day, sports fans, ties in with tonight's major upset of the only undefeated college team in the country, the number-one team in everybody's book, mighty Southwestern University.

"Southwestern, as you know, won the NCAA championship last year, the preseason National Invitational in New York this year, and has already been seeded number one for the national tournament that begins next Monday. Welcome to March Madness!

"The team that upset Southwestern tonight is currently in the news, dead center in fact: State University. State humbled the mighty champions after Southwestern ran up a winning streak of forty-eight consecutive games.

"The expected duel between two of the country's all-American stars, William 'Chip' Hilton of State University and Sheldon Kinser of Southwestern University, developed into a one-sided affair when the State University captain scored forty-two points to his rival's seventeen points.

"With that, let's pay some bills. We'll be back in two minutes with more collegiate basketball. Coming up: the sports story of the day that just might be the forerunner of the sports story of the year."

"You think he means us?" Soapy asked in delight. "It must be us! We're the big news!"

"Not yet," Chip warned.

"Whaddaya mean, 'not yet'?" Soapy demanded loudly. "We beat the best team in the country, didn't we?"

"It's not enough, Soapy," Chip said slowly.

The sports reporter came back on and continued. "Now, basketball fans, more of the story of the day. This story concerns sportswriters; newspaper editors; basketball reporters; members of the NCAA Selection Committee; its chairman, Tom Merrell; Ned King, the commissioner of the Midwest Conference; and certain college presidents. This announcer and hundreds of others have been bombarded with telegrams, letters, E-mails, and phone calls by fans out of University regarding the ability of their team. All this fervor was stimulated by the elimination of State University from consideration as a participant in the national tournament.

"Be sure to get this, because here is the big story. The commissioner of the Midwest Conference, Ned King, and the athletic directors of Northern State and A & M held a meeting yesterday afternoon just before the game at Archton. It was decided, now get this, *decided,* that in fairness to all teams in contention, the conference would be represented by the champion or not at all.

"This means that State University is still in the running for an invitation to compete in the national tournament. It was further decided that should Northern State and A & M play to a tie in the conference standings, the championship would be decided by the toss of a coin. Sanity and fairness prevail—"

"Whoopee!" Soapy yelled. "Whoopee! All right, baby!"

"Shhh!" Chip urged excitedly.

"In light of the fact that Northern State defeated A & M last night, the Northerners could, of course, win the championship by defeating State at University on Saturday night.

"State could win the title by defeating A & M Friday night at Archton and Northern State at University on Saturday night. If this was confusing for me to report to you, imagine how confused the selection committee must feel right about now. And now for the latest in women's collegiate basketball . . . ."

"Yes! Hooray!" Soapy yelled at the top of his voice. "Yippee!"

The phone rang, and Soapy leaped then to his feet and rushed to answer. He grabbed the receiver sputtering, trying to talk and listen at the same time. "Yes, sir—did you?—yes, sir. Right here, sir."

Soapy covered the receiver and extended it to Chip. "It's Coach Stone," he hissed. "He wants to speak to you."

"Hello, Chip," Coach Stone said excitedly. "Did you catch the news?" Instead of waiting for Chip's reply, he plunged on. "It's good news. Great news! Northern State and A & M wouldn't accept the NCAA bid. All we've got to do now is get Branch back in shape! Right? Well, get some sleep, if that crazy redhead will let you sleep. Good night."

"What did he say?" Soapy demanded.

"He said to get some sleep, if you'll let me," Chip teased.

"Is that all? Wasn't he excited or happy?"

Chip nodded. "He was excited, all right, but let's hit the rack anyway."

"Sure, Chip, sure. I've got just one little bit of writing left and then I'll turn out the light."

"You'd better not let Coach Stone catch you with the light on," Chip observed. "He's liable to see what you're up to."

"Aw, Chip, he's got stars in his eyes tonight. He wouldn't see me if I was hanging from the chandelier in the middle of his room."

"That's just where you'll be hanging if anyone finds out you're the person who has been sending all those messages."

Soapy grunted disdainfully. "Huh! How are they gonna find out? Here! You try it. My secret symbol is right here on this letter. I'm gonna send this to Mr. Star on Saturday night right after we knock off Northern State. Read it!"

Chip took the note and read it carefully.

SAM STAR
SPORTS DEPARTMENT
NORTHERN TIMES

ROSES ARE RED,
VIOLETS ARE BLUE.
NORTHERN PLAYED DEAD,
WHY DON'T YOU?

"You didn't sign it," Chip said.

"Well, not exactly."

"I don't see a symbol either."

"It's there. When we win the national championship, I'll show you a copy of everything I've sent. It's on every one of them."

CHAPTER 12

"Last Call"

COACH MIKE STONE was seated at a small table with his assistant coaches in the dining room, each of them absorbed in a newspaper, when Chip came down to breakfast. Neither Doc Terring nor trainer Murph Kelly was in sight, but some of the players were already eating breakfast at the team table. Chip walked over to the coach and asked if he had any news about Branch.

"He's about the same, Chip," Stone said softly. "As soon as the fellows finish their breakfasts, let me know. I want to talk to them." He surveyed Chip a moment as if to add something. Then he shook his head and resumed his reading.

Chip sensed that Coach Stone was strained; something had emptied him of the previous night's joy. All the coach's exuberance had vanished. Filled with apprehension, Chip walked over to the team table and passed the word that Coach wanted to talk to the team after breakfast. A few minutes later, after everyone had eaten, he caught Coach Stone's eye and nodded.

Stone folded his paper, walked slowly across the room to the team table, and waited patiently until the players were comfortable. "I have some bad news," he said abruptly. "Murph Kelly took Branch back to University this morning. Doc Terring will join us shortly."

The coach paused for a moment. Then, choosing his words carefully, he continued. "I know this is a tough blow for you. I assure you, it was a difficult decision to make. However, I felt that Branch should have the best possible attention.

"We can't possibly provide him with the treatment he needs while we're on the road. At home, in our own medical center, under the care of the university medical staff, there is an outside chance he may be ready for the Northern State game on Saturday."

There was complete silence. Not a player moved. Chip's heart sank. He wasn't alone when he said a silent prayer for Branch's recovery. He could only guess at the feelings of his teammates. How much could this team take?

He allowed himself one moment of self-pity. Then Chip firmly cast the depressing thoughts out of his mind and got to his feet. "It was the right thing to do, Coach," he said. "The only thing. Branch means more to us than *any* game. We just have to fight a little harder and a little longer now. Not only for ourselves but for Branch too. We've been in tougher spots, but we've never given up. Well, we're not giving up now—not when we've come this far."

"We'll kill 'em!" Soapy cried.

There was a murmur of assent from the rest of the players, and Dom Di Santis expressed all their feelings right down the line when he said, "We've always fought as a team. We'll fight as a team now." He bunched the powerful muscles of his arms and shoulders and shifted forward in his chair. "I'll be your big man tomorrow night, Coach."

Stone glanced swiftly at the determined faces. "I thought this would be your reaction," he said, a wide smile crossing his lips.

"All right," he said, his manner changing. "We've got some work to do. Let's get to it!"

Stone was all action now, all business. "Andre!" he said briskly. "I want everyone in the lobby at ten o'clock. Kelly's first-aid kit and his training bag are in the luggage-check room. Get them. You and your crew will have to double up as managers and trainers for the rest of the trip, but don't worry, Doc Terring will be traveling with us shortly. Let's get going!

"The rest of you pack up and review the A & M scouting notes. I've made some changes in our plans. We'll go over them on the trip. All right, that's it."

Chip and his teammates had looked forward to a restful flight to Archton, a brief workout that evening, and a relaxed shoot-around on Friday right up to game time. But Coach Stone was calling the shots, and he had other ideas.

Friday evening in their room, Chip and Soapy readied their uniforms and reviewed their scouting notes. Then, while they waited for Andre to call them for the trip to the A & M Field House, Soapy reviewed the events of the past two days.

"*This,* I'm going to frame," Soapy said, holding up the schedule Stone had created for them. "Listen! 'Thursday: On the plane. One! Each player to write a summary of the A & M attack and defense. Two! Each player to list the strengths and weaknesses of each of the A & M players. Three! Each player to report to Coach Stone personally and explain items one and two.' Are you listening, Chip?"

"What else can I do?" Chip bantered.

Soapy glared at Chip. "Well," he said, "you tell me a better way to keep our minds off the game. Anyway, here's the rest of it. 'Thursday. 3:00: arrive in Archton. 3:45: workout in A & M Field House. 6:00: dinner. 7:30: strategy session and video previews. 9:30: review offensive and defensive game plans. 10:30: lights out!

"'Friday. 9:30: wake-up calls. 10:30: brunch. 11:30: strategy session. 3:00: light snack. 4:00: rest. 6:00: bus to field house for the game. 6:30: trainers tape ankles. 7:00: dress. 8:00: pregame shooting practice. 8:25: return to locker room. 8:28: return to court. 8:30: tip-off time. 11:30: catch flight to University.'

"Now I ask you," Soapy moaned, "is that a schedule or is that a schedule? Well?"

"It's what we do," Chip said, suddenly feeling weary.

"Right! Are you still with me?"

"Where can I go?"

Soapy glowered at Chip for a moment. "I'll let that go," he said condescendingly. "Now, if my professors said I had to spend this much time on my classes—"

The telephone interrupted Soapy, and he rushed to answer. He nodded. "OK. I'll be right down." He cradled the receiver. "It's Andre," he said. "It's time to go. He said to bring our luggage."

During the trip to the A & M Field House, Chip thought ahead to the game. A & M was State's big rival, in all sports. Year after year, the two teams battled through every game as if each contest were for the national championship. Football provided the keenest competition, but basketball was a close second.

His thoughts shifted back to their first basketball game against A & M in the current season. It had been played at University, and Chip had been on the ex-athletics list, but Branch had played in that game. Phillips had given Roberts, the big Aggies center, a real battle.

Dom Di Santis was only six-five. At this level of play, no one could give away five or six inches to a good pivotman like Roberts. Dom would need help, Chip realized. But how?

The A & M Field House was packed to the rafters with cheering, jeering students and fans. The Aggies' fans had all turned out to see their team knock the Statesmen out of the running for the conference title. Besides, A & M had not yet conceded that it was out of the running for the championship. A win tonight would mean a lot. If the Aggies won tonight and the Statesmen bounced back and stopped Northern State on Saturday, A & M could tie for the conference title. Then the simple toss of a coin might put them in the national tournament. This was March Madness at its best!

The scent of victory was in the air, and the fans were prepared to do their part in cheering their team to victory. Mike Stone made no attempt to fire up his Statesmen. It wasn't necessary. Every player knew what the winning or losing of this game meant.

Di Santis lined up at center opposite Roberts, and Chip winced as he compared their heights. Dom was big and tough and willing. But, compared to Roberts, he was just a big "little" man. Chip was in his usual backcourt position, teamed up with Jimmy. Slater and Hunter were in the forward spots.

The crowd noise was at its peak when the referee tossed the ball in the air. Chip had sized up A & M's formation and figured Roberts would tap the ball forward, toward the Aggie basket. Following his hunch, he took a chance and left his opponent unguarded, darting between him and the jumping circle. The gamble paid off. The ball came straight to him, and he gathered it in easily. It was a good start.

Chip dribbled into his frontcourt spot and started the shuffle. Stone wanted Di Santis to keep Roberts moving in an attempt to wear him out. State's passing count went to eight before Jimmy Chung drove around his opponent. Jimmy stopped on the right side of the lane and went up in the air for his jumper. The shot was good, and State led by two points.

The Aggies brought the ball slowly up to their front-court to give Roberts time to gain position and jockey into a good scoring spot. Di Santis was trying to play in front of Roberts and immediately drew a foul. The big A & M center stepped out-of-bounds to receive the ball from the official for the throw-in after the foul on State.

Without hesitating, Roberts passed the ball to Najera, the cutting guard. In one continuous motion, Najera took a single hard dribble and then pulled up for a short jump shot that dropped cleanly through the hoop for two points. A & M evened the score at two each.

Jimmy and Chip advanced the ball upcourt and again went into the shuffle. This time it was Chip who broke free for the score. State was now two points ahead.

The Aggies advanced cautiously and after three or four passes got the ball into the pivot. Roberts hooked the ball over Di Santis's head for the score. The teams traded baskets evenly, but little by little, the Aggies pecked away until they passed the Statesmen and forged ahead. State stuck doggedly to the shuffle, fighting for every point and following Stone's game plan to the letter. The score at the half: A & M 39, State 34.

Andre Gilbert and his student managers took over the training duties, passing out the sliced oranges and Gatorade and checking injuries. Mike Stone studied his first-half notes for a few minutes and then reviewed the second-half strategy. Just before sending them out on the floor, he added, "It might interest you to know that Northern State has two scouts here tonight. Coach Brannon and his assistant are up in the stands. I hope they get an eyeful."

Chip grinned to himself. Brannon hadn't seen anything so far that he didn't know about the Statesmen. But the coach of the Northerners was sure going to get another look at the whirlwind press that had turned his team's play upside down at Northville.

The start of the second half was a duplicate of the first. Chip again stole the ball on the throw-in from midcourt. This time he anticipated a pass to A & M's big corner man and beat him to the ball. Once again, Chip started the shuffle offense. The Aggies continued to play their usual game, centering their attack around Roberts. With eight minutes left to play, A & M was leading, 51-46.

Then Di Santis committed his fifth personal foul as Roberts's shot attempt bounced off the rim. The Aggie scorekeeper sounded the buzzer several times to alert the official that Dom was out of the game. Coach Stone substituted J. C. Tucker for Di Santis, Speed Morris for Slater, and Bitsy Reardon for Hunter. Waiting until play was about to be resumed, he called for another time-out.

Chip could scarcely restrain a chuckle as he looked around the team huddle. State's team didn't even average six feet in height! Jimmy was five-ten, Speed was five-eleven, Tucker was a little over six feet, and Bitsy stood five-nine. Chip's six-four made him the tallest Statesman in the huddle, but his four teammates could run with lightning speed and they were tireless. Besides, all were absolute dead shots and constantly alert for interception opportunities. State's pressure game was about to get underway.

When play resumed, Roberts missed the first free-throw attempt, but he sank the second one, giving his team a six-point lead. Chip took the ball out-of-bounds and passed to Jimmy. The fleet dribbler was off! He passed to Speed and then the ball went to Bitsy and back to Jimmy at the top of the State free-throw circle.

Stopping there, Jimmy faked a shot. When the guard on the right charged him, he hit Bitsy with a crisp bounce pass. The little guy scored easily.

The A & M captain took the ball out-of-bounds and found each of his teammates covered by a Statesman. A wild heave downcourt resulted in an interception, and this time it was Chip who was unguarded when he scored.

The Aggie captain again took the ball out-of-bounds. He tried to hit a teammate under the State basket, but Chip, playing possum, started up the court at a leisurely pace and then suddenly whirled and, with perfect timing, intercepted the ball. Unopposed, he laid the ball against the backboard for State's third straight unanswered basket. The tally tied the score, and the frantic A & M coach angrily called for a time-out.

The delay didn't help. State had the Aggies on the run, and their lead increased steadily. Many of the fans left before the end of the game.

The final score: State 71, A & M 62.

All the hurrying and scurrying resumed as soon as the Statesmen reached the locker room. They had just thirty minutes to catch the bus to the airport. The Statesmen cheered and yelled and slapped one another around on the run. They were on their way to the warm bus as soon as everyone showered and dressed. In the meantime, however, the locker room was a madhouse of players and managers stuffing towels, uniforms, and warm-up suits into their travel bags. Within just a few minutes, bundled up with scarves around their necks and thick coats pulled over their State University blazers, the victorious team bounded onto their bus. They were going home to University at last!

With traffic in Archton heavier than expected, the bus was late reaching the airport. The coaches, players, and managers scrambled off the bus and ran into the terminal. They raced to the group check-in counter, lined up their bags, and received their boarding passes. Then each player scurried to the gate at the end of the concourse. When Chip looked up at the monitor along the way, he noticed the words "Last Call" flashing next to their flight number.

"Hurry up," he called out to Soapy, who had stopped to pick up a newspaper in the gift shop. "You'll miss it!"

"I'll be right there, Chipper," Soapy replied cheerfully.

"OK, see you on board." Chip disappeared through the doors and into the jetway.

Once on the plane, Chip glanced at his boarding pass and found his seat assignment put him next to Speed. Within moments, the warmth of the cabin and the rolling motion of the plane backing from the gate lulled Chip to sleep.

"Chip. Chip. Wake up, man. It's time for food," Speed nudged him in the ribs.

"Hey, thanks, Speed," Chip rubbed his eyes as he looked around the cabin. "Where's Soapy sitting?"

"Beats me. Just enjoy the quiet he's giving us for once," Speed joked.

Chip glanced over the rows in front of and behind him, but he didn't see Soapy. *Maybe he's in the bathroom?* he wondered.

He waited a few minutes, and when Soapy still hadn't appeared, he unbuckled his seat belt and walked up and down the narrow aisles.

Worried now, Chip checked with Bitsy and then with Andre. Neither had seen Soapy since they raced through the concourse to the gate. Chip walked up and down each aisle once more, but still there was no Soapy.

CHAPTER 13

Loyal and Dedicated

ANDRE GILBERT met Chip in the aisle by the rest rooms at the rear of the plane and looked questioningly at his face. "Any luck?" he asked worriedly.

"No, Andre. I couldn't find him."

"Man, do you suppose he missed the flight?"

"He must have."

Andre scratched his head. "Well, at least we know he didn't get off. One of us is going to have to tell the coach," he said tentatively.

"I'd rather be sure."

"Tell you what!" Andre said. "I'll walk through the cabin again, and you do the same, and if neither one of us finds him, then we can tell Coach. All right?"

Chip nodded and started looking closer at the dozing passengers. If Soapy wasn't on the plane, Coach Stone was going to hit the ceiling. Andre and Chip met back in five minutes. One glance at the manager's face was enough for Chip. He slowly got prepared. "Thanks, Andre," he said. "I'll tell Coach."

Stone was checking the scorebook when Chip caught his attention. The coach gestured toward the vacant seat across the aisle and tapped the book. "It makes good reading when you win," he said, smiling. "How do you feel?"

"All right, except for Soapy."

"What's wrong with him? Is he ill?"

"He isn't on the plane."

"What? Isn't on the *plane!* Where is he?"

"Back at the Archton Airport, I guess."

"Oh, no! That redhead is going to be the *death* of me. How in the world could he have missed the plane?"

"You know Soapy, Coach."

Stone nodded and sighed deeply. "Yeah, I know him. That's the one big mistake of my coaching career—knowing Robert 'Soapy' Smith."

"I know he'll have a good explanation," Chip urged.

"He'll explain, all right," Stone muttered.

"I hope you won't be too tough on him," Chip said hesitantly. "Soapy's really a great guy. He makes a lot of mistakes, but his heart and soul are tied up in the team. He loves basketball."

"I guess you're right," Mike Stone said thoughtfully. "Frankly, though, I don't think much of his basketball ability. But, as you say, he is loyal and dedicated. No team ever had a better morale builder."

"He keeps everybody happy," Chip added.

Stone eyed Chip for a moment. "You and Smith are pretty tight, aren't you?"

"We sure are," Chip said. "We've been friends ever since we learned to walk, I guess."

"All right," Stone said decisively. "I'll let it pass. You'll probably see him before I do. Suppose you tell him to forget it. But I still want to know where he was and how in the world he missed a direct flight to his own school."

Chip breathed a sigh of relief. Soapy was off the hook

for the time being. He thanked the coach, said a silent prayer, and went back to his seat next to Speed.

"So where's Soapy this time?" Speed chuckled, arching his eyebrows.

"Somehow he missed the plane, Speed, or he got on the wrong flight or something. Last time I saw him, he was at the gift shop buying more newspapers."

"That's our Soapy. What a clown. Does he try to do these things or do they just happen to him?" Speed continued. He handed an airline meal box to Chip. "Here's the sandwich and chips you missed when you and Andre were out scouting for you-know-who."

"Thanks, Speed."

"Say, you don't think he's flying the plane, do you?" Speed offered.

The longtime friends' eyes met for an instant, and then they both shook their heads and convulsed in laughter. In unison the two exclaimed, "No way! Not even Soapy!"

As Chip finished his dinner, his teammates walked the length of the cabin, laughing and talking about the game. Chip and Speed headed to the back of the cabin to join Dom, Jimmy, Bitsy, J. C., and Rudy, who were all arguing about the strategy Northern State would use in Saturday's crucial game.

"They'll hold the ball," Dom said.

Speed disagreed. "Uh-uh!" he said. "That's Coach's game. Brannon will try something tricky. Don't you think so, Chip?"

"I don't know, Speed," Chip replied. "Coach Brannon certainly knows what *we* can do. What *he* will do is anyone's guess."

The argument continued until the "fasten seat belt" signs were illuminated throughout the cabin. They all found their seats and prepared for their arrival in University.

The flight attendants opened the cabin doors as the passengers quickly cleared the overhead bins, gathered in the aisles, and walked toward the jetway. Chip was still wondering what exactly had happened to Soapy when he and Speed caught sight of the United Airlines ground employee just inside the gate area holding a small signboard marked "CHIP HILTON." Other players joked as they passed and asked if Chip had ordered limos for the team's arrival.

"I'm Chip Hilton."

"We have a message for you from our staff in Archton, Mr. Hilton." The man extended a folded note toward Chip.

Speed looked over his pal's shoulder. "Maybe it's about Soapy," he commented.

Chip quickly unfolded the note.

To:	Mr. William Hilton
From:	Mr. Robert Smith
Re:	A Funny Airline Rule
Date:	Basketball Season

Dear Mr. Hilton,

Did you know that all the airlines have this crazy rule?

"If passengers are late to the gate, the plane don't wait!"

(Even for little ole me!)

I'll arrive on the next flight to University. Please tell Coach I'll explain as soon as I get in.

SS

"Well, mystery solved. He missed his team flight! A first even for one Robert 'Soapy' Smith. Probably he was talking to someone in the gift shop," Speed announced, shaking his head.

For all their joking about Soapy, they were both relieved to know their childhood friend from Valley Falls was safe and would arrive home later on.

Chip hadn't expected anyone to meet them at that early hour in the morning, but when the team walked toward the baggage claim, the whole area was crowded with enthusiastic State University fans. In fact, the crowd couldn't have been more enthusiastic if the Statesmen had won the national championship!

Varsity cheerleaders, the student jazz band, and some of the members of State's big marching band combined their yells, music, and cheers to create a unique and deafening noise. Chip followed Coach Stone, and the first thing that caught his eye was Branch Phillips's head sticking up above the crowd. The big player caught Chip's eye, waved, and started moving toward him through the crowd.

Chip tried to get to Branch, but the fans wouldn't let him through. They grabbed him and lifted him to their shoulders. It was a full five minutes before he could get down and reach Branch. The big center was yelling as hard as anyone in the crowd, and when Chip reached his side, Branch gave him a bear hug, coiled a long arm around his shoulders, and lifted him off his feet, travel bag and all. It was then that Chip noticed Dr. Mike Terring standing just behind Branch. Chip shook the team physician's hand as he and Branch walked through the exit doors.

"How is your back?" Chip asked anxiously.

"It's still stiff," Branch said, "but Doc Terring has given me a back support—kinda like a brace—and he said I could play if I was careful. What happened last night? The announcer said you ran them off the court, said you got forty-seven points."

Chip told Branch about the full-court press and how Jimmy, Bitsy, J. C., and Speed had worked out against the Aggies. He was still talking about the game when the fans caught up with him again. The Statesmen were escorted to their bus at the curb. Chip noticed several cars, pickups, and SUVs decorated with red and white pennants. Many had signs adorning their doors, all extolling the prowess of State University basketball.

Minutes later, with horns blaring, the "parade" rolled slowly along Main Street and back to the campus, ending at the student union. The celebration started all over again and would have continued indefinitely if Coach Stone and his staff had not ordered the players inside for breakfast. After the team finished eating, Doc Terring and Murph Kelly asked the players about their injuries. Then Coach Stone directed them to get some rest.

Biggie Cohen gave Chip and Speed a ride to Jefferson Hall. Both players gratefully headed for their rooms and sleep. Chip was just dozing off when Soapy arrived. The redhead launched into a long story about stopping at the Internet cafe at the Archton Airport to send more E-mails. The girl at the counter had held him up. She didn't have change, and he couldn't leave without paying. Yes, she was pretty, but, no, he hadn't stopped to flirt with her. Yes, it had been a mistake. Soapy's main concern was Coach Stone's reaction.

Soapy sighed with relief when Chip told him that everything was all right but that Coach did want to see him. They slept until noon and then jogged down to Grayson's. They intended to get in a few hours before the afternoon shoot-around, but George Grayson sent Chip and Soapy home to rest.

Chip was glad to get away from the store and back to Jeff. University was hoop crazy. Thousands of fans were trying unsuccessfully to get tickets for the game. He and Soapy rested until late in the day. When they reported to the locker room, they felt rested and fit.

There wasn't an empty seat in Assembly Hall when Chip led the Statesmen out on the floor. Tonight the cheers were all for Chip and his teammates, and they responded with dash and spirit.

Tension was at a feverish pitch when the game began. A conference championship was at stake, as well as the invitation to play in the national tournament. The Statesmen and the visitors wasted no time in making their matchups and lining up for the tip-off. Each team was eager and ready.

Coach Stone started Phillips at center, Di Santis and Slater at the forward positions, and Jimmy and Chip in the backcourt. Branch was taped up, but it didn't affect his leap. He got the tap, Di Santis got the ball, and State went right into Stone's shuffle offense.

After the required seven passes, Chip hit Branch with a high pass near the basket. But the Northern State center, Todd Callihan, had Branch covered, and the ball came right back to Chip. The visitors were using a switching defense and trading opponents on every cross, and it slowed up Stone's screening attack. The Statesmen kept at it, and after a few more passes, Slater broke free for a shot. He missed the short jumper, and then the Northerners had the ball.

The visitors advanced slowly into their frontcourt and went into a pattern offense. Their big man, Callihan, took a position near the free-throw line. His four teammates cut in front of him and from corner to corner in a continuous roll attack.

The rolling continued until it became monotonous. It was pass and go to one corner, come back up the side of the court and get the ball, pass it off, and go to the other corner, over and over. The Statesmen were now getting a dose of their own medicine. The Northerners weren't going to let the Statesmen have the ball without using up all possible ticks on the shot clock.

With each Northern possession, Chip began to count the passes, and after a time, so did the fans. Someone started to count in the front row of spectators, and eventually a few fans close by joined in. Then it spread to a section and eventually to the entire side of the court. Soon the counting with each Northern possession reached every fan in the building.

Jimmy tried for an interception, and his opponent cut and scored. State came down and started the shuffle, passing and screening over and over, always waiting for the good shot. Chip got a three-point opportunity and hit one from about twenty feet out. Then it was Northern State's turn to play cat and mouse.

The fans didn't like it and began to count passes for both teams. There was no change, no break in the steady, monotonous pattern each team was following. The players began to feel the strain of the patterns, but no one weakened. Each team kept up the slow, deliberate attacks, all through the opening half. The score at half-time: Northern State 31, State 28.

The second half was a repeat of the first. Both teams were taking it slow and playing for a point at a time, as if each basket meant victory. Not a single fast break had been attempted by either team, and not one player had faltered in the slow, even pattern of play. Neither team could take a commanding lead as a result. The Statesmen would forge ahead, but then the Northerners would come right back and even up the score.

Branch tired badly late in the second half, so Coach Stone called for a time-out. After a short talk with the big center, Stone reluctantly sent J. C. Tucker in to replace Branch. Right then, as if Phillips had been the key, fatigue caught up with the Statesmen. This was their third clutch game in four days, and the tension and suspense had zapped their strength.

Chip saw it coming. It was etched into the tired faces of his teammates. He tried to show the way and call on a final reserve, but it wasn't there. He, too, was dead tired.

The Northern State players recognized the signs. When play resumed, they began to apply the pressure. They were fresh and strong and hadn't played for a week. They sensed the kill, sharpened their passes, drove a little harder, and pressed a little tighter on the defense.

Di Santis was matched against Callihan, but he wasn't big enough or strong enough to contain the six-ten pivotman. Callihan scored two consecutive baskets, which put Northern State out in front, 63-59.

Coach Stone sent Branch Phillips back in the game. The suspense was piling up and began to tell on both teams as each second slowly ran off the game clock. It was State's ball, and there were two minutes left to play when Stone called for another time-out. Standing in the huddle, he looked anxiously at the clock.

"I'm ready to try the press," he said worriedly. "A foul right now would be disastrous for us, so be careful. We've got ten team fouls, so each foul by us would give Northern two free-throw attempts. They're in the same boat as we are on fouls." It was a tough decision to make. He debated a moment and then put the question to the players. "What do you think, men?"

No one answered. Stone turned to Chip. "You're the captain," he said. "What do you think?"

Chip studied the clock. Two minutes left to play. The scoreboard read Visitors 63, State 59. Two minutes was a long time in a high-scoring game, but not in this kind of a contest. He pondered a moment more and then reached a decision. "I think you're right. We should use the press, Coach."

"All right," Stone said firmly, "the press it is!" He turned to the bench. "Morris," he called. "Report for Slater. Reardon! You're in for Phillips."

When Speed and Bitsy returned from the scorers' table, Coach Stone gave them their final instructions. "We press right after we take a shot, whether it goes in the hoop or not. We need the ball. Get it!"

Chip took the ball out-of-bounds and waited for the official's signal to play ball. The referee blasted his whistle, and Chip passed inbounds to Jimmy. His backcourt partner drove quickly into State's frontcourt and waited for the teammates to get set. The Statesmen had discarded the shuffle now and were using their give-and-go game. The tempo of the game had shifted in favor of State University.

After a few passes, Jimmy got the ball back. He snapped it to Chip and cut for the basket. Chip faked a return pass and, when his guard lunged forward to stop the pass, cut around him and went up for his jumper. It hit! Now they were only two points behind, with still a minute and a half to play.

Chip charged forward, following the ball. He was right behind his opponent when the ball fell through the net. His opponent took the ball out-of-bounds, and Chip played him tightly, windmilling his arms and trying to deflect the inbound pass. But Di Santis didn't cover Callihan in time, and the big center got the ball.

Both teams failed to score on their next possessions. Northern managed to pull down the next shot, which State University missed. Seconds continued to drain off the game clock.

The visitors tried to kill time now, to eat up the full ten seconds in their own backcourt and to use the full thirty-five seconds on the shot clock. The Statesmen were putting on a last-effort man-to-man press now; they dogged their opponents all over the court, and the Northerners couldn't get the ball into their frontcourt in time. The official whistled out the violation and gave the ball to State out-of-bounds at midcourt. The fans went wild. State's defense had kept them in the game, and now it would be up to the offense to seize the moment.

Coach Stone immediately called for a time-out. When Chip walked over to the sideline to join in the huddle, the game clock showed twenty seconds left to play.

The score: Visitors 63, State 61.

"Listen, men," Stone said, his voice shaking, "this is the most important basketball play you will ever make. It's our last chance and it's got to work. Chip! You take the ball out-of-bounds. Di Santis, Speed, and Bitsy: You three set the pick for Jimmy. It's our twenty-six play.

"Don't botch it up, or else you kiss everything you've fought for good-bye. You can do it, men!"

CHAPTER 14

From
the Line

CHIP TOOK the ball out-of-bounds on the side of the court, and Dom, Speed, and Bitsy set the triple screen for Jimmy. The little guy faked right, cut left, and drove his opponent smack into the screen. Jimmy then broke into the clear, and Chip bounced the ball to him. At the same time, Callihan, the visitors' big center, switched to cover the play. But he was behind Jimmy, so Chip breathed a sigh of relief.

Then, just as Jimmy went up to release the ball for the lay-in, Callihan made a tremendous leap with his long arm snaking across and above Jimmy's head. The ball never reached the backboard. Callihan slapped it away at the last second, and the ball flew straight into the hands of the visitors' big corner man. He zipped the ball up ahead to the visitors' playmaker. At the same time, the other backcourt teammate broke out of the screen and raced toward the visitors' basket.

Chip had cut upcourt for defensive balance and was caught all alone in a two-on-one situation. He cast a despairing glance at the clock and backtracked with every ounce of strength left in his legs.

If ever a play had backfired at the wrong time, this was it. Back he went, and on came his two opponents, passing the ball from one to the other.

There was no help in sight. Jimmy's lay-in leap had carried him off the court, and he was standing under the State basket as if paralyzed. Dom, Speed, and Bitsy had been facing the Northern State basket, watching the play, and Callihan's unexpected save had caught them flat-footed. They started forward to press when Callihan stopped Jimmy's shot, but the visitors' tall corner man had passed the ball over their heads and toward the Northerners' goal. They turned then and raced back to help, but they were too far back and clearly out of the play.

Chip knew it was now or never. There were only seconds left to play, and some kind of a move had to be made. Fast! He faked toward the taller player just as he passed the ball to the playmaker. "Now!" he gritted, springing directly in the path of the playmaker. Chip was gambling that the little speedster would try to get rid of the ball in a hurry, perhaps try a bounce pass to his tall teammate. It was a desperate chance, but he had to take it!

Straining down as far as he could, Chip stabbed at the ball with his right hand just as the player bounce-passed the ball. His extended fingers got a piece of the ball, and it went spinning crazily away, toward the visitors' goal. Chip and his two opponents were after it in a flash, with all three converging on the ball in a desperate charge.

Chip got there first and made another stab at the ball. He hit it! A fast tap brought it under control, and then he was off, but he was dribbling in the wrong direction, away from the State University basket. Both

Northern players were right behind him, one on each side. He couldn't turn, and he knew they were bent only on making a desperate dive for the ball. They were willing to risk any penalty if they could stop a play.

The crowd noise was deafening, but Chip heard Jimmy clearly yell. He cast a quick glance back over his shoulder. Jimmy was all alone under the State basket, screeching, yelling, and leaping in the air, all the while waving his arms. Chip's opponents had him boxed in, and in another second it would be too late. He dribbled once more toward the visitors' basket, leaped high in the air, and hooked the ball far back over his head. It took off in a long, lazy curve, but it was on its way!

He saw Jimmy move a step closer and take a lightning fast glance at the clock. The little fighter leaped in the air and tapped the ball toward the basket with both hands. Chip saw the ball fly up in the air, and he heard the buzzer end the game. At that precise second, the two Northern players crashed into him, burying Chip under their bodies.

Right then, the greatest outburst of sound Chip had ever heard seemed to lift Assembly Hall right up off its foundation. He crawled forward and looked at the scoreboard just as a big "63" rolled into place under the State sign to match the "63" under the Visitors sign.

The two Northerners who had crashed into him clambered to their feet. Chip made it to his knees. He remained there for a second and checked the scoreboard once more to make sure he hadn't imagined it. There it was, 63-63. The score was tied! State's hopes were still alive, and lots of things could happen in an overtime period.

He got to his feet and started toward the sideline feeling a rush of relief. He never made it to the bench. Jimmy, Speed, Dom, and Bitsy mobbed him and led him toward the State University basket.

"The ref called a foul! Those guys fouled you!" Jimmy shouted. "The referee called a foul."

"You can win the game!" Bitsy echoed. "You've got two free throws coming."

The fans were going wild. Chip looked toward the bench. Soapy was halfway out on the court, yelling like a maniac and heading straight for him. Coach Mike Stone had the redhead by the shirt tail and was trying to yank him back to the bench. The rest of his teammates were leaping up and down, and Andre Gilbert was methodically throwing towels and the Statesmen's warm-up jackets in the air, stooping to pick them up, and hurling them aloft again.

Then it struck home. Jimmy's basket had tied up the score, and he could *win* the game—*if he could make the free throws.*

Chip's strength was coming back. Still, he was far from ready when he reached the free-throw circle. The referee handed the ball to him, but the fans were still yelling and cheering, and he stepped back from the charity stripe for a moment. It was an excuse to delay the shot and to relax a bit more.

The noise quieted then, so he moved forward to the line. He checked his feet to make sure they didn't touch the free-throw line, bounced the ball four times against the floor, and focused his eyes on the ring. He jiggled the ball with his fingertips and slowly unlocked his wrists. Then he flexed his ankles up and flipped the ball toward the basket with a full follow-through. His right hand extended his follow-through—first his fingers and then his whole shooting hand dipped into the basket. It seemed like a perfect finish to a free-throw shot and a perfect ending to the game.

The ball went spinning toward the basket, twirled down, and spun off the rim, bouncing sadly on the floor. The fans held their breath as the official again handed

him the ball. Chip toed the line for the second attempt.
Without hesitating, he followed the same well-practiced
process. This time the ball snapped through the ring,
rocked once in the net, and fell happily through the basket to win the game and the conference title. The score:
State University 64, Northern State University 63.

The crowd erupted into bedlam. Speed, Jimmy, Bitsy,
and Dom lifted Chip on their shoulders, and he saw
Coach Stone and Soapy waltzing around and around.
The players from the bench joined the players surrounding him a split second before the fans swarmed out
of the stands to flood the floor in a surging torrent of
wildly excited and happy people.

Someone hoisted Jimmy up beside him, and the
crowd paraded the two State players across the court
and as far as the players' aisle. Chip got down and, with
Jimmy beside him, led his teammates in a mad charge
for the State locker room.

Andre Gilbert couldn't find the key, and he turned
out his pockets and began tearing off his red and white
SU sweater to check his shirt pocket for the key. Murph
Kelly came along, calm, cool, and efficient as always, and
opened the door. Despite the trainer's protests, the
Statesmen put on a locker room celebration to end all
celebrations.

The Northern State captain came by, and Andre let
him through the door long enough to extend his congratulations. Mike Stone arrived just then, and they
hoisted him up on Kelly's trainers' table and called for a
speech.

The happy coach was far from prepared to talk sense
right then, but he did say that he didn't see how Chip
ever got that ball away from the two Northerners and
that Jimmy's shot was the prettiest he ever saw in his
entire life and that Chip's free throw was the most
important he would ever make and wasn't it a lucky

thing it was Chip who had to shoot the free throw instead of, well, say, Soapy Smith.

Chip felt completely rested then, and joined in the yelling, speech making, and handshaking. At the height of the celebration Dad Young arrived, accompanied by several photographers and sportswriters. Stone bellowed for silence. "Dad Young has an important announcement to make," he shouted.

Soapy moved over beside Chip and Speed, and the three of them waited side by side for Young to speak. Chip felt sure he knew what Young was going to say, but he forced the hope out of his mind.

Mike Stone was holding up both arms for silence, and his eyes were shining. "Quiet!" he yelled. "Quiet! You're going to like this!"

That quieted them and they crowded forward. Dad Young held a fax and waved it in the air before speaking. "This," he said, "came this afternoon following a phone conversation I had this morning with Tom Merrell. It says, 'The winner of tonight's game is invited to represent the Midwest—'"

That was as far as he got. The players crowded around him and slapped him on the back and shook his hand and, to Murph Kelly's disgust, lifted him to the training table.

The big man was smiling and obliging. He complimented them for an uphill, underdog fight that only a real championship team could make. He concluded by saying, "Several weeks from tonight, just about this time, I expect to be in San Francisco, accepting the first national basketball championship trophy State University has ever won."

The photographers took pictures and the sportswriters asked questions and made notes. The Statesmen hit the showers as soon as they could get away gracefully. By the time they were dressed, only the players, Murph

Kelly, Andre Gilbert, and Coach Stone and his assistants remained. The coach called for their attention and then discussed plans for the tournament.

"We practice tomorrow afternoon. It's Sunday and you should be able to get plenty of rest. You are expected to attend your Monday morning classes and then report here at one o'clock. We're leaving for Chicago at two o'clock, so be on time. Somebody be sure to tell Smith!

"By the way, we play the second game Monday night, so we will try to get in some extra shooting practice before the first game. We come back the same night. Congratulations again. Remember, eleven o'clock curfew tonight and tomorrow night. That's all." He glanced at his watch. "That gives you thirty minutes to get home. Get going."

Chip, Soapy, and Speed struck out for home. On the way they passed the student union, where Soapy told Chip and Speed to go on ahead. "I've just got to get a snack, and I might even send an E-mail to Sam Star," he said smugly. "This is something I've been looking forward to for a long, long time. Star is going to love this one."

Chip groaned. "Oh, no! Here we go again."

"Nope!" Soapy said happily. "This is positively the last. And," he added, "the best."

Practically all of Jeff's residents were waiting for them when Chip and Speed arrived at the dormitory. They were anxious to start another celebration, but they relented when Chip told them Coach had said they had to be in bed by eleven o'clock.

The reaction had set in, and Chip was exhausted. He undressed and was just dozing off when Soapy arrived. The redhead quickly got ready for bed and turned out the light. Chip was sound asleep in five minutes, and Soapy soon followed. When Chip woke up the next morning, Soapy was writing quietly at his desk. The Sunday papers were stacked unopened on the dresser.

"What are you doing?" Chip asked curiously.

"I'm doin' some figuring . . . working on an out-of-bounds play."

Chip propped himself up on both elbows in bed and stared at the redhead. It was the first time ever Soapy had passed up the Sunday sports pages. "What about the papers?" he asked. "What about the articles on the game?"

"Aw, I know those by heart. I read them at the union. Listen! I'll give you the headlines. 'State turns back Northern State to gain spot in NCAA tournament.' 'Pairings for NCAA tournament now completed.' 'State to represent Midwest Conference in NCAA.' 'Southwestern is the team to beat in top-talent NCAA.' 'Never a greater extravaganza than State-Northern battle.'"

Soapy paused. "Good enough?"

"There must be more than headlines," Chip teased.

"Of course! All the papers carried stories on the game. Get this: You got 44 points for a season total of 799 points. That gives you a game average of 38 points per game compared to Kinser's total of 847 points and an average of 38.5 points per game." Soapy paused again.

"Will that hold you until you get dressed?" the redhead chirped.

"I guess so," Chip said. "Why all the sudden interest though in out-of-bounds plays?"

"Because we could have lost the game on that out-of-bounds play we tried to work last night just before the end of the game."

"I suppose you can work out a better one," Chip needled with a yawn.

"I know I can. The fact is, I've got one worked out. It's foolproof."

"Show me. We've got some time before we leave for church."

"All right. Just imagine the same situation we had last night. We've got the ball out-of-bounds on the side of the court, there are three seconds left to play, and we're behind by a point. Got the picture?"

"Yep."

"I take the ball out-of-bounds, and you stand close to the basket but on the other side of the lane. That means your guard will play in front of you, between you and the ball. Right?"

"I suppose so. Go ahead."

"Well, I look back toward the other team's basket and make out like I'm going to throw the ball in that direction. That's different, huh?"

"It sure is," Chip agreed dryly. "Especially since it wouldn't fool too many people."

"Just wait! I fake a throw to the backcourt and then I turn like a flash, and I throw the ball as hard as I can against the backboard right above the basket. It rebounds over the head of your guard and right into your hands, and then you lay it right back up against the backboard and we win the game. Pretty good, eh?"

"So far so good. What makes you think you can hit the backboard just right every time?"

"Because I can throw to second base from behind the plate and knock the base runner's cap right off his head. I oughta be able to hit that great big backboard. Here! Take a look at it. I've got it all drawn out."

Chip studied the drawing for a moment and then handed it back. "It might work," he said thoughtfully, "if it isn't against the rules."

"It isn't. The other team gets the ball if it hits the *back* of the backboard from out-of-bounds. But the rules say it's OK if the ball hits the *front* of the board from out-of-bounds. And there's lots of time. Besides, everybody knows that time doesn't start until the ball touches a player on the court. This play is foolproof! It can't miss."

"Maybe not," Chip said kindly, "but you better check with a basketball official."

"I'm doing better than that," Soapy said triumphantly. "I'm writing to the top official in the game, the rules commissioner himself!"

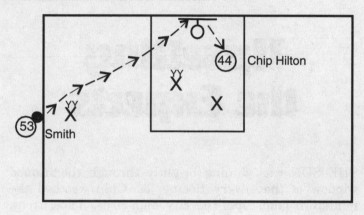

CHAPTER 15

Upsetting the Experts

THE SUN was shining brightly through the framed window of the silvery Boeing jet. Chip watched the miniature landscape: the city high-rises, fields, trees, fences, houses, interstates, and mall complexes down below. The glistening surface of the ice-covered snow was too much for his eyes though, so he closed them and relaxed, enjoying the warmth of the Sunday morning sun as they took off from Chicago O'Hare Airport and headed for University.

His thoughts flew back over the events of the past several weeks. He was beginning to understand what was meant by the term "March Madness." It seemed impossible that so much could have been crammed into such a short span of time. With Chicago as the Midwest Regional playing site for the NCAA Tournament, the Statesmen's travel consisted of flying back and forth between, with University as the home base.

On Wednesday afternoon they had traveled to Chicago for their game with Ohio State. To their surprise, they had won handily on Thursday night, clearly outplaying the representatives of the Buckeye State. They had been excused from classes in University on Thursday and Friday and had met Oklahoma on Saturday night. Again the Statesmen rolled over the opposition. Now they were in the "Sweet Sixteen."

They had returned to University on Saturday night after the game. The team spent Sunday and Monday at home before departing again on Tuesday afternoon to prepare for their Thursday night contest against Kansas.

They had earned their way into the "Elite Eight" of the national tournament by beating Kansas in overtime. Chicago remained "home" to the Statesmen as they worked out for their Saturday evening game against Syracuse. The winner of that game would advance to the NCAA Final Four in San Francisco.

The game against the always well-coached Syracuse team went back and forth right down to the final moments. With just five seconds left in regulation time, Speed's alert rebound of Jimmy's missed three-pointer sealed a State victory, 72-70.

Only four teams remained in the sixty-four-team national tournament. State University was one of those special "Final Four" teams. The Statesmen would now spend a day or two at home before flying to the West Coast.

Soapy was sitting in the seat opposite, mumbling to himself and busily clipping basketball stories and scores out of the Sunday papers. He grunted with satisfaction and leaned across the aisle to tap Chip on the knee with a handful of clippings. "Listen to this!" he said. "Come on, you're not asleep. Are you listening?"

Chip opened his eyes and nodded. "Yes, I'm listening."

"This is a headline: 'Southwestern University, West Virginia University, Texas Tech University, and State

University gain final spots in NCAA championships.'
Sounds good, eh?

"Here's one you won't like: 'Southwestern committed
enough miscues to lose the game in last night's big win
over Connecticut, but the champions were good enough
to overcome their mistakes and gain a spot in the semifinals.' Here's the story," Soapy announced.

"'In the third quarter, "Two Ton" Bordon connected
twelve times in twelve attempts from his favorite spot
in the pivot. Within arm's length of the basket, the big
fellow used space-eating leaps and his height and
weight to overpower Connecticut's Ted Smith. Smith,
at six-seven, was three inches shorter in actual height
but far taller in basketball know-how and stature.
There doesn't seem to be any way to stop the SWU
giant.'

"What do you think of that?"

"Branch stopped him. That's what I think, Soapy,"
Chip smiled.

"Right!" Soapy agreed. "Listen to what they say about
us. 'One of the most exciting and hair-raising college
basketball games of this tournament was played last
night as State triumphed over Syracuse, 72-70. The dra-
matic triumph of finding a way to win when games get
tight has become a habit with the Statesmen.'

"Only two more to go," Soapy exulted. "Now here's
something about you. 'State's Chip Hilton has scored
32, 39, and 33 points in the first three tournament
games to bring his season total to 903 tallies in
twenty-four games for an average of 37.625 points per
game.

"'Southwestern's Sheldon Kinser has also played in
twenty-four games but has scored 916 points for a game
average of 38.166. Both players are sure of two more
games now that the NCAA has chosen to reinstate the
consolation game before the final two teams square off.

Should one of the teams be defeated in the semifinal round, the scoring opportunity will be present for Kinser or Hilton in the consolation game.'

"You're gonna beat him out, Chip. I just know it. You're gaining every game. Listen to what Joe McCallister of *Sports Illustrated* said about you!

"'Chip Hilton, the State Spaceman, has unstoppable drive and possesses deadly accuracy with his jump shot. Kansas's Tom Corrs had the unenviable job of guarding Hilton last night. The Kansas defensive star had this to say: "Hilton is the toughest man I ever played. You never know what he's going to do until it's too late. He can change direction on a dime and has deadly accuracy from any spot on the floor. He's an uncanny passer, and if you try to double-team him, he'll find his unguarded teammate every time. I don't think there's a player in the country who can hold him."'"

"What do you think of that?" Soapy asked.

"It's a lot of nonsense . . . just like your out-of-bounds play."

"It's not nonsense, and you and Stone are gonna be the first to admit it."

"Coach didn't seem to appreciate it at practice the other afternoon," Chip teased, glad the subject had changed.

"Aw, Chip, he thought I was foolin' around. You wait until I hear from the rules commissioner."

"If he answers such a crazy letter."

"He'll answer it," Soapy said confidently. "If he says it's OK, will you practice it with me? We can go over to the Y a couple of times and get it down perfect. OK?"

"All right," Chip agreed, "but I still don't see why you're so sure you can hit the backboard just right. Especially when you're going to fake a throw somewhere else."

"I've been doing a little secret practicing," Soapy said gleefully. "Every time I go through the park, I practice with rocks or snowballs. I can hit the right tree every time."

"I hope so," Chip observed.

"I've practiced with a basketball too," Soapy said indignantly. "I'm just as accurate! You know where I got the idea?"

"Nope."

"Well, you remember the time back in high school when we were studying parabolas and the trig teacher hit me with the eraser?"

"I remember," Chip said. "He conked you right on the top of your head."

"It didn't hurt," Soapy reflected. "It was a soft eraser, but that's not the point. He threw it from the front of the room clear to the back of the room, and he hit me square on the top of the head. Right?"

"That's right."

"You know what he told me?"

"Nope."

"Well, he said he knew all along I was the one creating the noise when his back was turned and he was writing on the blackboard."

"How strange," Chip said, trying not to laugh.

"Aw, Chip, let me tell it. Anyway, he told me he practiced after school until he could turn and throw the eraser right over the top of my desk. Every time."

"So!"

"So, I've been doing the same *thing!* I've been trying it with rocks and a basketball every chance I get. I even paced off the distance from the sideline to the backboard so I would throw the right distance."

There was more. When Soapy got started, he was hard to stop. Chip sighed with relief when the pilot announced their approach into University. He got his things together and in a few minutes, the plane pulled to a stop at the familiar terminal.

The gate area was full of well-wishers again. If anything, there was a bigger crowd on hand, and this one was just as enthusiastic. Mr. and Mrs. Grayson and Mitzi were waiting in their usual spot. Chip and Soapy eventually made their way through the crowd and reached them.

"Where's Cara?" Soapy asked abruptly.

Mitzi answered the question. "She hasn't been to work for several days, Soapy."

"Is she sick?"

"I don't think so."

Soapy put on a good act on the ride to Grayson's, but Chip knew he was worried about Cara. He was too happy, too effusive; Soapy put on too good a show.

Mr. Grayson was thrilled with their success in the tournament and said so. "It's good for business," he said briskly.

Everyone laughed at that observation. The store stood on its own feet when it came to being a successful operation, despite George Grayson's frequent assertion that the athletes drew customers. Grayson's was one of the largest retail stores in the state and, in addition, served as a distribution center for a great number of items that were shipped to bordering states.

Mitzi, Chip, and Soapy got out of the car at the store, and the Graysons continued on home. Inside, Chip stopped at the cashier's desk to talk to Mitzi. Soapy headed straight for a phone.

"What's wrong with Cara?" Chip asked.

"I think it's got something to do with her father."

"Maybe he's sick."

"No," Mitzi said, "I've seen him going to work every day. In fact, he's been working late almost every night. I've seen him on my way home after work."

Chip walked back to the stockroom. Skip Miller and Lonnie Freeman grabbed him as soon as he opened the door. "Some game!" Skip cried.

"Great job, Chip!" Lonnie agreed. "We watched every second of each game here at the store. You should've seen the way this place was packed. We even taped the games for you guys. The announcer was bragging before the game how that Kansas guard, Tom Corrs, was going to shut you out. Way to show them all!"

"Look at the tournament bracket sheet," Skip said excitedly. "We've hit it right on the head so far. Take a look!"

With his two assistants pressing close beside him, Chip walked over to the desk and studied the tournament chart pinned on the wall. The two boys had carried State all the way through to the championship on the chart.

"Did you see that I wrote in the names of the winners?" Skip asked excitedly.

"We know who's going to win the championship," Lonnie said quickly, "but we're hoping West Virginia beats Southwestern."

"You can never tell with those Mountaineers," Chip said. "They have a way of upsetting the experts. Don't count them out yet."

Soapy entered the stockroom so quietly that the two high schoolers didn't hear him. Chip was watching for his friend and turned as the redhead closed the door. One look at Soapy's face was all Chip needed to realize that Soapy was not only down but down-and-out.

Skip and Lonnie sensed something was wrong, but they passed it over and greeted Soapy with congratulations, handshakes, and slaps on the back. The two teenagers were Soapy's greatest admirers. Soapy tried hard to assume the happy-go-lucky attitude the youngsters liked, but it fell flat. He was hurt.

Chip wanted to reassure Soapy but wasn't sure what to say. He turned back to his desk and got busy with some paperwork, hoping Skip and Lonnie would take the hint and give Soapy a chance to work out his problem.

At closing, just after the last group of customers filed out of Grayson's, a dejected Soapy Smith slumped down in the chair next to Chip's desk in the stockroom. "Cara won't hardly talk to me, Chip. I know something must be wrong at home. I really want to help, but she won't tell me what's going on and doesn't want to talk about it. She just says it has nothing to do with the two of us."

Chip nodded and said quietly, "Sometimes families need to work through their problems, Soapy. I'm sure when the time is right, she'll tell you what she can and ask for your help. So maybe the best thing to do is to pray about it and respect her wishes."

As he followed a more contented Soapy Smith out Grayson's front door and into the cold night, Chip Hilton never for a moment considered that he would be the one asked for help.

CHAPTER 16

A Matter of Urgency

MITZI HANDED a letter to Chip when he arrived at the store after Monday's practice. "This came for Soapy," she said. "Where is he?"

"He stopped up the street. I think he wanted to call Cara from an outside phone. Have you heard from her?"

"No, not directly."

"But you know what's wrong," Chip persisted.

"Not exactly. Frankly, I think it has something to do with her father."

"You said he was working though, right?"

"I don't mean illness," Mitzi said thoughtfully. "Somehow or other I gathered it was something about his business. Cara said he had been working day and night. He's the executive vice president, you know. That's an important job."

"There isn't anything wrong with the savings and loan association," Chip said calmly. "Mr. Grayson is on the board and he says it's as strong as First National Bank."

"I really don't know," Mitzi said honestly. "I was just guessing."

"Let me know if you find out anything, will you? Soapy is all upset. He said Cara wouldn't talk about it, whatever it is."

Mitzi nodded. "I know. Cara and her father are really close. I'll let you know if I hear anything."

Chip didn't think about the letter until he reached the stockroom. He glanced at the envelope. It was from the president of the International Association of Approved Basketball Officials. "Soapy will be glad to get this," he mused aloud. "Maybe it will cheer him up."

He pondered a moment. "Or maybe it won't." Anyway, it will be a diversion.

Soapy came in a few minutes later, and Chip handed the letter to him. "Here's the answer to your out-of-bounds play," he said.

"Now we'll find out how the ball bounces."

Soapy opened the letter and glanced quickly down the page. "Yes," he said, "it's legal." He handed the letter to Chip and sat down by the desk.

"Aren't you happy about it?" Chip demanded. "What's the matter with you?"

"Cara. What else?"

"What's up?"

"She said there was some kind of trouble in the family. She said she wouldn't talk about it and that she didn't want me to call her for a while."

"Well, we've got plenty to keep us busy," Chip said eagerly, anxious to change the subject and cheer up his pal. "Let's get back to this out-of-bounds play."

Chip noted the heading on the letter and then read it from beginning to end. Soapy had been right on all counts.

INTERNATIONAL ASSOCIATION
OF APPROVED BASKETBALL OFFICIALS
John P. Nucatola, President

Dear Mr. Soapy Smith,

The answers to your recent questions follow:

Question 1: Legal play. Goal is good. (Rule 7-6 ques.)

Question 2: If time is out on the throw-in, time starts when the ball touches a player on the court.

Question 3: It is assumed, according to your diagram, that player 53 is out-of-bounds in his team's frontcourt. If so, the ball must be handled by an official. (Rule 7-6; 9-3)

I hope I have made the answers clear. It is an extremely unusual play, and I have never seen or heard of it having been used. However, according to the present rules, it is perfectly legal.

Sincerely,
John P. Nucatola
President

"Now will you practice it?" Soapy demanded with a grin.

"Sure," Chip said quickly, eager to please his pal.

"Anytime?"

Chip nodded. "Anytime you say."

"Let's do it now. Cara's got me all mixed up."

"Come on," Chip said briskly, turning toward the door. "We can use the court at the Y before their evening programs begin." He locked the stockroom door and took the lead. Soapy loved action. The out-of-bounds play might be just the ticket to get Cara Davis out of his pal's mind. At least for a while.

At the gym, Chip got a ball and permission to use the floor. Downstairs, when they reached the court, he let Soapy take charge. Soapy took a position out-of-bounds on the side of the court, and Chip walked to his position under the basket.

Soapy faked a pass toward the backcourt, turned swiftly, and pegged the ball on a direct line to the backboard. The ball hit directly above the hoop and dropped down into Chip's hands. "Now do you believe it'll work?" Soapy cried triumphantly.

Chip grinned and nodded in defeat. The redhead's throw had been perfect. Practicing a play like this, however, with just the two of them present, was very different from executing it against an opposing team and before thousands of fans. One throw proved too little.

Soapy must have read his thoughts, because the redhead suggested they try it again. "I can do it every time, thanks to math class and Rockwell's coaching at Valley Falls," he boasted.

And he did! He threw the ball a dozen times and every peg was a bull's-eye. Soapy was back on an even keel again. He made Chip feint with his eyes, had him look back upcourt as if expecting a backcourt teammate to take the throw-in, and had him turn back to the board just as the ball came whizzing toward the basket.

Chip humored Soapy all the way. But he couldn't help thinking that the practice was all a waste of time except for the fact that it had taken Soapy's thoughts off of Cara. On the way back to work and even trudging through the snow home to Jeff after work, Soapy talked about nothing except his play, "Soapy Smith's SOS Special."

Chip had no classes Tuesday until ten o'clock, so he spent the time studying. He was still worried about losing his place on the dean's list. During the hectic first semester when Grayson's illness had tied him down at the store, he had been unable to find enough time to take care of his job and basketball. He had tried to do too much, and his studies had suffered. Later, while Chip had been on the ex-athletics list, he had regained much of the lost ground. He wanted to make sure he kept up with his studies and handed his assignments in on time.

The pressure and tension of the coming weekend began building up at practice Tuesday afternoon. Chip could sense it in Coach Stone's voice and actions and in the nervous behavior of his teammates.

At the end of practice, Stone called them together and gave them the final trip instructions. "We fly out at eight o'clock tomorrow morning. Everything has clicked so perfectly the past week that I'm scared to death something is going to happen. Button up your overcoats and wear hats. Don't even breathe too deeply!" he said, trying to keep his voice light.

"I'm hoping we can get on our way in good health and in one piece. And," he added pointedly, "for goodness' sake, don't miss the plane. Got that, Smith?" That brought a laugh from everyone, and Stone ended the session.

Chip and Soapy checked in at the store right after practice. Mitzi waited until Soapy was out of hearing and reported that there had been no word from Cara. She did draw attention to the sports page of the *Herald*. Chip went back to the stockroom and read sportswriter Bill Bell's column. The first line, the topic sentence, established the keynote:

> *In the heart of the young, defeat is only a*
> *preliminary to tomorrow's victory.*

Bell then discussed the Holiday Invitational Tournament and how it had brought about the development of a great new center, Branch Phillips. Then he explained the difficulties new coach Mike Stone had encountered and how the challenges had broadened Stone's coaching philosophy. He discussed the illness that sidelined Chip Hilton and noted how his return solidified team and coach unity. He then outlined how the players had responded to the privilege of observing their own training rules and strong attendance at practice.

Chip liked Bell's closing sentence:

> *It all adds up to ultimate victory whether or not the Statesmen ever win or lose a national championship.*

Skip and Lonnie came in just as he finished reading Bell's column. He put the paper aside and outlined the work to be done during his absence, but he could sense that he wasn't getting through to them. Both youngsters were thinking of nothing but the tournament.

Wednesday morning, Chip, Soapy, and Speed ate an earlier-than-usual breakfast with their Valley Falls friends, Red and Biggie, at the student union. Then the three players met the team at Assembly Hall for the short bus ride to the airport. The rest of their teammates were already there, surrounded by a group of fans. As soon as they arrived, Andre Gilbert counted heads and told Coach Stone everyone was there. A few minutes later the bus pulled away, accompanied by the cheers and good wishes of the fans.

Once on board the airplane, Chip settled into his window seat next to Speed and dozed all the way to Chicago. Coach Mike Stone, taking no chances of leaving anyone behind, was seated on the aisle and had securely penned Soapy in next to him in the window seat. After a short layover at O'Hare, the State University team lined up to board the last leg of its cross-country flight to the NCAA Final Four in California.

Walking down the ramp to the plane, one man turned to stare back at the Statesmen. He was wearing dark glasses and seemed vaguely familiar to Chip. But he turned away before the young star could get a good look at his face. Chip quickly forgot about it.

The passengers moved slowly into the plane as flight attendants checked tickets and directed people toward their seats. There was the usual flurry of action: hoisting items into the overhead bins, reading magazines, and adjusting seat belts. The "fasten seat belts" sign flashed on, and the pilot made his last-minute announcements as the plane made its way onto the runway. The big plane taxied slowly out on the runway, crawled forward for a short distance, and then swept along the glistening asphalt at lightning speed. Moments later the jet was in the air, nearly a thousand feet above the airport and climbing.

The flight attendants served beverages and snacks almost as soon as the plane was airborne. Chip enjoyed the window view and Soapy seemed his old self for a while—even with his new seatmate. But when Chip finished his snack, he noticed the redhead had lapsed back into unnatural moroseness.

Later, Chip studied for an hour or so and decided to take a nap. He glanced at Soapy. His teammate was sound asleep.

Sometime later he was awakened by the pitching of the plane. The inflight crew was checking seat belts, and a few of the passengers moved restlessly and complained, but Soapy never made a move. When the redhead went to sleep like that, it meant he was thoroughly exhausted. It would take more than a storm to bring Soapy back to consciousness. Chip glanced at the bright flashes of lightning that ripped through the storm clouds. He turned on his side and tried to sleep.

A few minutes later, one of the crew tapped him on the shoulder. She checked her passenger list and asked if he was William Hilton. He nodded and she asked him to join her in the aisle. Surprise was evident in his eyes, but the woman only tapped her lips with a finger and beckoned him to follow. Completely mystified, he loosened his seat belt, stepped carefully over Speed, and reached the aisle.

"We have a gentleman on board by the name of Davis," the attendant said. "He is very ill and wants to see you. Do you know him?"

"The only person I know by that name is from University," Chip said. "It could be him."

She led Chip to the rear of the plane and stopped beside a man who was leaning forward. Evidently he was suffering a great deal of pain. It was the man he had seen in the boarding line! The man looked up just then and glanced at Chip. It was Mr. Davis, Cara's father.

Chip gazed at Davis in shocked surprise. His face was ashen, his lips dry and white. Heavy lines were etched into his brow, and all the blood and life seemed to have drained out of him. There was a vacant seat beside him and Chip sat down. "Is there anything I can do, Mr. Davis?" he asked.

"I don't know, Hilton," Davis managed through set teeth. "It's my stomach. A terrible pain! I can hardly stand it." He clasped both arms around his stomach and bent over until his head touched the back of the seat directly ahead.

Chip felt completely helpless. The flight attendant returned, and he moved out into the aisle so she could sit down beside Mr. Davis. The calm crew member tried to question the man, but Landon Davis was in such pain that she could learn nothing except that he had never had an appendectomy or evidence of a heart ailment.

She got to her feet and motioned for Chip to remain. "I'll get the captain," she whispered. "I think it's his appendix or a heart attack. Please stay with him."

She was back in less than a minute with the captain, and he waited patiently while she took Mr. Davis's temperature. When she removed the thermometer from Mr. Davis's lips, she held up four fingers and eyed the captain with concern.

"All right!" the captain said decisively. "We'll put down at Denver. I'll call ahead for an ambulance to meet us at the gate." He turned to Chip. "Are you a friend of his?"

Chip nodded.

"I think he's going to need your help," the pilot said.

"I'll be glad to do all I can," Chip replied.

Landon Davis looked up and nodded his thanks. Then he leaned forward and resumed his rocking, leaning forward and then slowly back, over and over. The flight attendant got Mr. Davis's coat, and a few minutes later the "fasten seat belts" sign lit up as the captain informed his passengers about the unscheduled stop for a medical emergency.

The plane began its descent, breaking through the foam of white clouds until the outline of the city below was clearly visible. The plane landed gently, taxied to the end of the runway, turned, and swept quietly and swiftly back to the airport terminal.

Mike Stone and some of the players sat up and looked around as the inflight crew moved along the aisle advising passengers that they would be taking off again immediately.

Davis seemed to realize for the first time that he was to leave the plane when the captain again joined the group. "What's the matter with me?" he asked.

"I think it's your appendix or gall bladder," the captain said kindly. "I imagine you will need immediate medical attention. We've called for an ambulance to meet you at the gate."

Landon Davis jerked upright but immediately clasped his stomach and leaned over again. "I can't!" he gasped. "It's impossible. I've got to get to San Francisco. It's a matter of the greatest urgency."

"So is protecting your life," the pilot said tersely.

Davis lifted his head until he could see Chip. "Hilton," he breathed hoarsely, "you've got to help me. Can you stay with me until I find out what's wrong? I can't begin to tell you how important it is."

Mr. Davis tilted his head back until he could see the pilot. "Can you get a later flight for Hilton? I'll gladly take care of any expense involved."

"That can be arranged easily enough," the captain said soothingly. "Don't worry about charges. Just relax." He turned to Chip. "Is it all right with you, young man? We'll unload your luggage."

"I'm with the State University basketball team," Chip said. "We're all together. I'll have to ask Coach Stone about staying with Mr. Davis."

"Let me talk to him," Davis pleaded.

"I'll take care of it," the pilot said quickly. He turned to the attendant. "Please ask Mr. Stone to come back here."

She went ahead, and Chip waited anxiously, hardly knowing what to think. One thing was for sure: He couldn't leave Cara's father sick and all alone in a strange city!

CHAPTER 17

Too Much at Stake

"EVERY SECOND is important," the surgeon said tersely. "But I can't do a thing until he gives me permission to operate."

The man's crisp voice cut through Chip's thoughts and brought him back to the grim reality of the cold, white walls of the emergency room, the wheeled stretcher on which Davis was lying, and the decision he must make. He glanced once more into Mr. Davis's tortured eyes. Chip couldn't hold back any longer.

"All right, Mr. Davis," he blurted out, reaching for the slip of paper and the money the sick man clutched in his hand. "I'll do exactly what you asked me to do. I promise."

It was done! He had made a promise, and he was committed. A brief smile flashed across Landon Davis's drawn lips, and Chip barely heard the faint thanks the desperately sick man whispered. Chip said a short prayer for him, then the attendant immediately wheeled the stretcher out of the room as Chip walked slowly back to the waiting taxi.

The Denver airport clock showed 12:30 when Chip got back to the terminal. His plane to San Francisco was scheduled to leave in forty-five minutes. He glanced at his watch and set it to California time. Back in University it was 2:30. The fax he had sent for Mr. Davis should have already arrived.

He sat down in an airport lounge chair and reviewed the events of the past few hours. It was almost unbelievable that all the bizarre things leading up to the situation in which he now found himself could have been crowded into such a short time.

Coach Stone had reluctantly agreed to let Chip accompany Mr. Davis to the hospital, but the coach had made the pilot promise to have Chip on the next plane to California. Chip could still hear Stone saying: "Chip Hilton means the difference between a national championship and an 'also-ran.' I must be crazy to even think of such a thing."

I must be crazy, too, Chip was thinking. Davis had been adamant. Although the surgeon had advised the man that he was risking peritonitis, Davis had obstinately refused to submit to the emergency appendectomy unless Chip promised to complete the errand that necessitated his trip to San Francisco.

"This is a matter of life or death too," Davis had said stubbornly. "No, there is no one else who can do it! No, there is no other way!"

Chip even suggested to Mr. Davis that Soapy complete the last part of the errand, but the man had reacted so violently to the suggestion that Chip had feared he was going to pass out altogether, right then.

Chip's thoughts shot ahead to San Francisco. Coach Stone would be awaiting his arrival, and he dreaded to think what the coach's reaction would be when he told him he would have to return to University. How had he gotten into this anyway? What a spot!

Chip knew how *he* would react if he were the coach. It would be too much to take. Mike Stone would be upset and indignant and suspicious and find it wholly impossible to believe that *anything* could be important enough to drag a Statesman player, especially the captain, away from his team just days before the State University team was to play in the NCAA Final Four with a chance to win the national championship.

The utterly impossible details Mr. Davis had recounted raced through his mind. As executive vice president of the University Savings and Loan Association, Davis was in charge of all the big loans. An important duty was completing the morning reports of delinquent payments.

It had all started when a lifelong friend, Bob Burnes, had borrowed sixty thousand dollars. Davis had vouched for the loan. He had known Burnes all his life, trusted him like a brother, and knew him to be absolutely trustworthy. The loan was as good as gold, but Burnes had run into difficulties that had held up his payments. To make it worse, Burnes had been forced to move to San Francisco in order to complete a big contract.

Davis had not included Burnes on the delinquent payments report for several weeks. He hadn't worried about the matter until a week or so before when he learned that the annual audit was soon to be made. He had contacted Burnes to make arrangements to have the money at the end of the present week.

The previous afternoon before Davis and Chip met in the plane, the sick man had learned that the auditors were expected Saturday morning. It was imperative that the funds be deposited and posted on the books before the office closed Friday afternoon at two o'clock.

Chip studied the slip of paper Davis had given to him. Bob Burnes lived at 300 Buena Vista Avenue in San Francisco. His private phone number was 740-2187.

Chip's task was to get the bank draft Burnes had, take it back to University, and give it to Mr. Davis's secretary, Barbara Burton. She knew exactly what to do. Mr. Burnes had promised to wait at his home until Davis arrived Thursday night.

Davis had been too afraid to trust the regular mail or overnight delivery services. There was much at stake: his job, his reputation, and, more importantly, his family's welfare. Cara and her mother had realized something serious was disturbing him, but they knew nothing about the loan, which was why he wouldn't ask Soapy to do the job for him.

If Mrs. Burton got the draft before two o'clock, everything would be OK. *Sure,* Chip thought, *but how about the team and my other commitments?* He was still worrying about Coach Stone and how he would explain his predicament. *Lord,* he prayed, *help me to know what to do.*

It was 2:15 in the afternoon when Chip arrived at the airport in San Francisco. He headed straight for the airline reservation desk. The ticket agent was understanding and friendly. When Chip told him who he was and how important it was for him to get back to San Francisco early Friday evening, the clerk checked all the airline schedules and worked out the best possible trip.

"Here you are," the clerk said, handing a card to Chip. "That's the best I can do."

FRIDAY

Flight 647   Depart SFO 3:30 A.M.   (Pacific Coast Time)
Arrive ORD 10:30 A.M.   (Central Standard Time)

Passenger to check with hotel for train/bus
schedules from Chicago (ORD) to University (UNI).

Flight 834   Depart ORD 6:45 P.M.
                    Arrive SFO 8:40 P.M.

"There's no flight service into University on Friday afternoon and none back to Chicago that will make your connections," the clerk said. "You'll have to use a train or bus, I guess."

"Have you got a train schedule?" Chip asked.

The airline agent smiled and shook his head. "No," he said, "I can't help you there, but I'm sure the manager at your hotel can look it up."

Chip paid for the plane tickets with the money Mr. Davis had given him and thanked the clerk. Then he took a taxi to the Sonesta Coast Hotel.

It was a long ride, and he used the time to think about getting back from University in time to make flight 834. Even if he *could* get a train or bus, it was going to be almost impossible to get back. He checked the trend of his thoughts long enough to wonder whether or not Coach Stone would even let him play if he did get back. He wouldn't blame the coach if he dropped him from the team.

The taxi pulled up in front of the hotel. He paid the driver and checked in at the desk. The clerk told him he was registered with Soapy and gave him a key. Before going to the room, he asked the manager to check the afternoon train and bus schedules from Chicago to University.

"No buses and only one train to University in the afternoon," he said. "It leaves at, let's see, now, it leaves at 10:30 A.M. Chicago time—that's 8:30 A.M. our time. Is that any good?"

"I think so. How about returning to Chicago?"

"Forget the buses again. They make too many stops. You'd miss the flight you're trying to make. There's no train after two o'clock."

That was a setback, but it wouldn't do any good to worry about it. His big job was to get to University and deliver the check and *then* figure out how to get back to Chicago. He walked to a phone booth to call Burnes.

He dialed the number and waited for the answer in an agony of suspense. Seconds later, a man answered and, to Chip's surprise, called him by name.

"Hello," Burnes said. "Is this William Hilton?"

"That's right," Chip said. "How did you know who it was?"

"Landon Davis called me from Denver just before he went into the operating room. The surgeon is going to call me later tonight, and I'll call Mrs. Davis. By the way, I have the certified check. Where are you?"

Chip told Burnes the name of the hotel and his room number. The man advised him to stay put. "I'll be there in less than an hour," he promised.

Chip's sigh of relief must have been audible to Burnes, because he chuckled with understanding. "I know just how you feel," he said. "I was afraid you wouldn't make it. Just stay right there."

On the elevator, Chip glanced at his watch and groaned. It was 6:00 P.M. San Francisco time and 9:00 P.M. University time. It had been a long day of traveling, but Chip was just getting started. When he reached the door, he inserted the key as quietly as he could, but Soapy heard him and switched on the light.

"What happened?" Soapy asked drowsily. "Where have you been?"

"I can't tell you, Soapy. It's strictly confidential."

Soapy sat up in bed and stared incredulously at Chip. "What's so secret about it?" he demanded. "Man, Chip, you can tell me."

"No, Soapy, I can't tell you or anyone else. I promised not to, and I won't break my promise. And that isn't the half of it. I've got to go back to University. Tonight."

Soapy's eyes opened wide in surprise. For a moment he couldn't grasp the meaning of Chip's words. "Tonight!" he gasped. "What for?"

"I said I couldn't tell you, Soapy." Chip opened his suitcase and pulled out some clean clothes.

"What about the game?"

"I'll be back. I've got to be back."

"I don't know how you're going to do it. Can't someone else go? Can't I take your place?"

"Nope."

"Why can't it wait until we get back?"

"Because there isn't time. I must get back to University by two o'clock Friday afternoon. That's all there is to it. Talking about it isn't going to help."

"You mean it's more important than the national championship?"

Chip nodded grimly. "Yes, it is. To me anyway."

"But what about the coach?" Soapy said. "What will he say?"

"I'm going to find that out in about five minutes," Chip said crisply. "And that, old pal, is going to be almost the hardest thing I ever did in my life."

Chip showered and changed clothes. Soapy was still sitting on his bed, bewildered and completely confused. He was hurt too. There had been few secrets between them. Chip felt a sharp twinge of regret. This kind of treatment wasn't helping the redhead's morale, but he was going to solve Mr. Davis's problem confidentially, as promised. If it snapped Cara out of her doldrums, Soapy would hopefully have her back in his life.

Soapy was still sitting on the side of his bed when Chip left the room. He had forgotten to ask for the coach's room number so he went down to the lobby and got it from the desk clerk. Then he called Coach Stone from one of the house phones.

Stone answered immediately. "I'm sure glad to know

you got here," he said. "I haven't been able to sleep thinking about it."

"I have some bad news," Chip said. "I don't know how to tell you, Coach, but I've got to go back to University right away. I have my ticket for what they call the 'red eye,' the 3:30 A.M. flight to Chicago and a return ticket that'll get me back here at 8:40 Friday night."

"You have *what!*" Stone shouted. "A ticket for where? Chicago? University?"

"That's right, Coach. I *have* to go back."

"What in the world for?" Stone cried. "What are you trying to do to me, drive me crazy? No, *sir!* Absolutely *not! Nothing* doing! It's impossible."

Chip waited until the coach finished. "I gave my word, Coach," he said quietly. "I've got to do it. There isn't any other way."

Mike Stone's voice was more reasonable now, but he was still bewildered. "Couldn't anyone else do it? Andre or a special messenger or someone like that? Why in the world do *you* have to make the trip? It doesn't make sense. It can't be that important."

"But it is, Coach. I know you will find this hard to believe, but it means more to me than winning the national championship. And I have to go myself . . . ." Chip hesitated a second and continued, "even if it's *without* your permission."

Stone said nothing for a long, long time. Chip knew he was trying to decide what to do. He wished he could help by telling the coach the entire story, but that wasn't an option.

"This is mixed up with that Davis guy, isn't it?" Stone asked shrewdly.

"Yes, sir, but it isn't because of him that I have to go. It's for someone more important. Someone I can't let down, no matter what the cost." Chip thought of how bewildered Soapy had looked when he left the room.

"How are you going to get back?" Stone asked.

"I'll make it!"

"*Coaching!*" Stone said, his voice filled with futility. "*Boy!* If I live through *this,* I'm going to get a job selling newspapers. Preferably someplace where they've never even *heard* of basketball."

He paused for a long moment. Then he sighed and said, "All right, Chip. Go ahead. *But for goodness' sake,* get yourself back here for the game! I'll handle the media as well as I can. Call me before you board your last flight, and I'll have Andre meet you."

Chip thanked Coach Stone and hurried back to the hotel room. All he needed now was the certified check. So far, so good.

CHAPTER 18

The Clinching Drive

CHIP HELD his hand over the pocket that contained the precious check and raced for the taxi line outside of Chicago's O'Hare Airport. He opened the door of the first cab, leaned in, and said, "I've got only forty-five minutes to get to the train station. Can you make it?"

The driver whirled around in his seat and studied Chip's anxious face for a second. "I think so," he said calmly. "Get in and hold your hat."

The man wasn't fooling. Although the streets were slippery and would have slowed an ordinary driver, the man at the wheel of the cab was an expert who drove swiftly and confidently.

"Where are you headed, young man?" the driver asked over his shoulder.

"University," Chip said. "I've *got* to make it."

"You will!"

From that moment until the taxi slowed down in front of the train station, Chip held on to the door handle for dear life. The meter showed $13.25 when the man began to slow down, but Chip didn't dare wait for his change. He handed the driver a twenty-dollar bill and was off and running before the cab came to a full stop. "Thanks a million, kid!" he called. "You're the greatest!"

Chip dashed across the broad concrete entrance under the great pillars and took a position in the shortest line standing at the information booth. It took only a few seconds for him to reach the head of the line, but it seemed like a lifetime. "Which track for University?" he asked breathlessly.

The man behind the counter jerked a thumb toward the end of the big lobby. "Track 34, son. Better hurry!"

Chip was on his way. He dashed under the arch just before the attendant closed the grilled steel door. The long platform was deserted except for a solitary trainman who was just swinging aboard the train. Chip turned on the steam and sped along the side of the train. He reached the opening and sprang through it just as the brakeman started to close the door.

"Where did you come from?" the conductor asked in amazement.

"San Francisco," Chip said. "Is this the train to University?"

"That it is," the man said.

"Do you think we'll reach University on time?"

"I think so," the man said casually. "We might be just a few minutes late."

Chip found an empty seat and dropped wearily into it. That had been close!

It was eighteen minutes to two on Friday afternoon when the train eased into the station at University. Chip was the first passenger off the train and ran to the taxi stand. A single cab was waiting. He leaped into the back seat and gasped out his destination.

"Sure! Hey, you're Hilton," the driver exclaimed. "Aren't you supposed to be in California?"

"I'm going right back. Please step on it."

The driver nodded and concentrated on his driving, covering the distance in less than ten minutes. Chip paid him and forced himself to walk casually across the sidewalk and through the entrance. As soon as he reached the lobby, he turned to the left and entered Mr. Davis's office. A young woman was seated at a small desk beside the door. She immediately rose to her feet. "You're Chip Hilton," she said eagerly.

"That's right," Chip said. "And you're—"

"Barbara Burton," the secretary said.

Without another word, Chip handed the envelope to her and glanced at the clock on the wall above her desk. It showed two minutes to two. Barbara Burton smiled and nodded understandingly. "Just in time," she said. "Everything will be all right. I'll call Mr. Davis and tell him. This is a wonderful thing you have—"

But Chip was gone, and Barbara Burton didn't know the half of it.

He walked swiftly up the street and turned in at Grayson's. Cara Davis was at the cashier's counter and looked up in surprise. She started to speak, but Chip beat her to it. "Where's Mr. Grayson?" he asked.

"In the office," Cara said. "What's going on?"

"Business," Chip said quickly, already moving in that direction. "Excuse me, please. I've got to see Mr. Grayson right away." He ran up the steps to the office.

Through the open door, Chip saw George Grayson sitting at his desk. Chip knocked lightly. His employer sprang to his feet in startled surprise. "Chip!" he cried. "What in the world are you doing here?"

"I had to come back on personal business," Chip said quickly. "Now I've got to get back to San Francisco in time for the semifinal game. I can make it if I catch my plane out of Chicago at 6:45 tonight. I thought you might be able to help me hire a local plane."

"Wait a minute," Grayson said. "Let me catch my breath." He sat down and thought for a moment. "What about the time?" he asked.

"We're three hours ahead of the West Coast," Chip replied quickly.

Grayson nodded. "That's right . . . let me see." He reached for the phone. Three calls were unsuccessful, and Chip's heart sank.

Grayson nervously tapped a pencil on the top of his desk and then made a sudden decision. "Last chance," he said. "Jack Binns is a personal friend of mine. He has his own plane. We're in if I can reach him."

After what seemed an interminable length of time, Mr. Grayson reached his friend. "Got him!" he whispered to Chip.

Grayson greeted Binns and got right to the point. He explained the problem briefly. Then, nodding his head from time to time, he listened to his friend. When Binns finished speaking, Grayson said, "Will do, Jack. See you at the airport at 3:30. Step on it!"

Grayson cradled the receiver and turned back to Chip. "Now," he said, "what happened?"

Chip told him as much as he could without violating Mr. Davis's confidence, and his employer seemed satisfied. Then he suggested that Chip check the stockroom while he made a few phone calls. "I've got to make arrangements for you to reach the airport from the private landing field Jack will have to use. I'll meet you out front at 3:15."

Chip went down to the stockroom and checked the order and arrival slips and then walked out to the front of the store. Cara was busy with a customer, but she held up an envelope and indicated that she wanted him to wait. When the customer left, she gave Chip the envelope. "For Soapy," she said eagerly. "Please give it to him."

Chip tucked the envelope in his pocket and promised to give it to Soapy as soon as he reached San Francisco. "If I get there," he added.

"I don't suppose you've heard," Cara said, "but my father had an emergency operation in Denver early this morning. He's doing fine."

George Grayson came along at that moment, and they left for the small, private county airport where Jack Binns kept his plane. They had been at the field only a few minutes when a small plane taxied over to the front of the terminal.

"That's him," Grayson said. "Come on."

They hurried out on the field, and Chip climbed into the plane. The two friends talked while Binns waited for takeoff permission from the tower. As soon as he got clearance, Binns said good-bye, taxied the light plane to a position at the end of the runway, and took off. Two hours later, at 5:30, Binns brought the plane down at a small airport on the outskirts of Chicago.

Chip thanked him and ran to the small building that served as both an office and waiting room. A man met him at the door and said he had been contacted by George Grayson with instructions to get a Chip Hilton to the Chicago O'Hare Airport by 6:45 P.M. "We'll have to hurry," he concluded.

It took a little over an hour to reach the airport, and again Chip took off running. There was just enough time to call Coach Stone and say he would be on flight 834 and arrive at 8:40 P.M.

Once in the terminal, the gate attendant glanced briefly at his ticket, tore off the airline portion, gave Chip the ticket stub with his seat assignment, and asked him to board. A few minutes later the plane moved out on the runway. It was soon in the air.

The flight attendant served a hot meal shortly after the plane leveled off, and Chip ate everything that was served. After he finished, he placed the tray on the empty seat next to the aisle and leaned back to rest. He was asleep in five minutes.

A long time later, someone touched him lightly on the arm. He came awake with a start. "We're coming into San Francisco," the crew member said gently, handing him his jacket. Chip looked out the window. It was growing dark, but far below he could see the lights of the city. The plane touched down on the runway with scarcely a tremor. A few minutes later, Chip was at the gate and headed for the nearest exit.

Andre Gilbert was waiting at the arrival area and led Chip excitedly toward a taxi that was parked just outside. They climbed in and the driver immediately drove away. Andre handed Chip's uniform to him. "You'd better put it on," he said, "Texas Tech is using a two-three zone, and we haven't got anyone who can hit from the outside."

"Soapy can hit," Chip said. "He's got a great set shot! So does Rick Hunter."

"They're not in uniform."

"Who's not in uniform?"

"Soapy and Rick. They had a fight, and Coach Stone wouldn't let either one of them suit up."

"What were they fighting about?"

"You! It happened last night in the locker room after practice. Rick said you were letting the team down. He said the team should come ahead of everything."

"Then what happened?"

"Soapy said if you went back to University, you had a good reason."

Chip nodded grimly. "He was *so* right."

"Anyway," Gilbert continued, "Rick said no one with any loyalty at all would leave his teammates in the lurch. That did it! Soapy flew at him like a tiger, swinging both fists. Naturally, just then, Stone came in and caught them. If you've ever seen anyone sore, it was Coach. He really got on Soapy. He said it was the last straw and he didn't care if Soapy packed his bag and went home. Right then!"

"Where's Soapy now?"

"Oh, Coach Stone said he and Rick could sit on the bench but couldn't dress. When I left, Soapy was sitting on one end of the bench and Rick was sitting on the other end."

The taxi stopped to make a left turn, and Chip saw the Cow Palace in the background. The driver drove through the heavy cross traffic and pulled up to the main entrance of the arena. The roar of the crowd could be heard from there.

Andre grabbed Chip's clothes and thrust some money into the driver's hand before leading the way at a dead run. Just as they ran through the entrance, the noise died down. When they slowed to walk through the aisle to the court, Chip saw that there was a time-out.

He glanced quickly at the scoreboard. There was less than a minute left to play and the Texas Tech Raiders led by two points, 74-72. His eyes shot ahead to the State bench. The first person he saw was Soapy. The redhead was sitting at the end of the bench nearest Chip, staring down at the floor.

Chip pulled Cara's letter out of his warm-up jacket pocket and held it in his hand. A fan recognized Chip just then and stood up and pointed toward him. He shouted Chip's name and began to yell something. Soapy leaped up and saw him and began to yell something at the top of his voice too. Now practically everyone in the arena was looking at him, and he could hear fans shouting his name. Chip handed the letter to Soapy as he passed. Then he joined the players circle surrounding Mike Stone.

The coach thrust out his big hand and pulled Chip into the center of the circle. "Tough spot, Chip," he said with great excitement. "I can't even give you time to catch your breath. Report for Tucker."

As Chip started away, he heard Stone yell, "Morris! Report for Phillips. Bitsy! Go in for Slater."

Chip walked to the scorers' table and reported. Speed and Bitsy arrived just as he turned to go back to the bench. On the way, he saw Soapy reading Cara's letter. The redhead was grinning. He looked up and caught Chip's eye and raised his hand in the air, forming the OK circle with his thumb and forefinger. Chip joined the circle, and Stone made sure they had their matchups. "You take number 33, Chip," he said. "He's a lefty and can't go right."

The five speedsters closed the circle around Coach Stone and clasped hands. "Press!" Stone said. "Right off the bat!"

They went out on the floor and lined up against their assigned opponents. The Texans had set up an out-of-bounds formation under the State basket, and number 33 took the ball out. Chip went into his jumping-jack routine, but the Tech player safely inbounded the ball and sped along the sideline.

State had applied the press, but the Texans had been ready for it. Safely across the ten-second line, they went into a freeze formation to use up time on the shot clock— passing to a teammate and cutting away from the ball each time, keeping the center of the court open.

The clock ticked the time away, and the Texans continued their passing. The game was nearly over, and the two-point lead was looking bigger and bigger as each solitary second dropped off the game and shot clocks. Chip and his teammates pressed as close as they could, forcing their opponents for all they were worth but trying to avoid a foul.

Then, with only seconds left to play, the Texans gave the ball to Chip's opponent and cleared to the other side of the court. Chip knew what that meant. Number 33 was going to drive in for the clincher. The Texan player felt the game was over, and he was going to show everyone how he could drive past the so-called all-American guarding him.

It was foolish basketball, and it backfired as senseless play almost always does. Number 33 faked right. Chip pretended to go for the deception, but when his opponent started his dribble to the left, Chip made his move, jabbed at the ball, and took it away. It was done so quickly that the Texan made one more dribble motion with his hand before he realized Chip now had the ball.

Chip drove for the State basket at full speed, and on the other side of the court, running three feet ahead of his opponent, was Speed. Speed had known immediately what to do when Chip went for the ball.

Chip gave his old Valley Falls teammate a long, floating football pass. The ball dropped lazily beyond Speed and bounced on the floor. Speed gathered it in on the run and softly laid it up against the backboard. His opponent tried to stop the shot, and Chip heard the official's whistle before he saw the ball drop down through the hoop.

It was a perfect three-point play. He glanced at the scoreboard. The score was tied, 74-74. Speed could win the game!

The teams lined up at the State basket. The officials waited for them to get set. When Speed got the ball, he didn't fool around. He aimed and jiggled and used his perfect shooting form to spin the ball up and out and down through the net without the ball hitting the rim. Chip backtracked and looked at the scoreboard, which read: State 75, Texas 74.

With two seconds left to play, the Texas coach called for a time-out. When play was resumed, the Raiders tried a long, full-court pass to their big center, but Dom and Chip both saw the play coming and went for the ball. They collided in midair. Chip got it and dropped down on the court right where he was. Doubling up, he circled the precious ball with his arms and body as the buzzer ended the game. State University was in the finals of the NCAA Tournament!

CHAPTER 19

Unknown Star Gazer

CHIP WAS RELAXING in a chair beside the window and thinking about Soapy. Behind him, sitting on the floor, the redhead was clipping sports stories out of the Saturday morning papers, commenting happily on those that referred to State. Cara Davis's letter had done the trick. The redhead hadn't said much about his trouble with Rick Hunter, but Chip knew Soapy, and he knew Soapy would blurt out everything in time.

"Listen to this," Soapy exclaimed. "'Mighty Southwestern enters the final stage of its quest for a third consecutive NCAA basketball crown tonight. The opposing finalist is upset-minded State University, which is the only team to defeat the champions (twice) in the past three years.' How's that?"

"Sounds all right to me," Chip grinned.

"How about this?" Soapy continued. "'Interviewed last night after his team defeated West Virginia University to gain a berth in the finals, Coach Jeff Habley, Southwestern's veteran mentor, said, and I quote: "If we don't beat State tomorrow night, I quit!'"

"He's out of a job and doesn't know it!" Soapy concluded delightedly. "Listen!

"'The game tonight will match two teams with every asset a champion needs. Southwestern has two all-American players and the nation's leading scorer. Sheldon "The Shot" Kinser leads the nation with 930 points in twenty-five games and boasts an average of 37.2 points per game. The powerful SWU squad possesses depth, height, power, and experience.

"'State University has one all-American player. William "Chip" Hilton ranks second in national scoring with a total of 903 points in twenty-five games for an average of 36.12 points per game. The great State star saw action for only one minute last night and failed to break into the scoring column. This left Kinser with a 27-point lead, an almost impossible handicap for Hilton to overcome.'

"Huh!" Soapy growled. "We'll see about that! Lessee now. 'These great scorers will battle it out nose to nose tonight for the scoring championship.

"'State does not have the depth of the reigning champions nor the overall height, but the team does have lots of speed. According to Coach Mike Stone, the Statesmen are at their peak for tonight's game.'

"Now listen to this one, Chip. 'When the members of the NCAA Selection Committee read the papers today, they will discover that State did exactly what the human dynamo predicted who originated the letter, E-mail, telegram, and phone campaign that flooded their offices. The unknown star gazer vowed the Statesmen would win their way to the finals of the tournament.'

"Zowie!" Soapy cried. "I'm a 'human dynamo'!"

The reference to the letters, E-mails, telegrams, and phone calls brought Chip's thoughts back to Soapy. The redhead had practically put State in the tournament. There were other considerations too. Soapy had to play in one more game to be eligible for his letter. One thing was for sure: The redhead wasn't going to get in the game if he wasn't in uniform. Chip decided to do something about that right now.

He leaped to his feet and put on his warm-up jacket. "I'll be back in a few minutes," he said.

"No, sir!" Soapy said anxiously. "I'll go with you. The last time I let you out of my sight you covered two thousand miles."

"Well, the last time I let you out of my sight," Chip teased, "you missed the plane! No, you stay here. I'll be right back, I promise!"

Chip took the elevator to the lobby and called Coach Stone. The coach told him to come right up to his room. A few minutes later he knocked, and Mike Stone opened the door. "Come in," he said. "Have a seat. I never did get to ask you how you made out on your trip."

"Everything clicked," Chip said.

"That isn't what you came up here to talk about though," Stone said, eyeing Chip knowingly. "It's Smith, isn't it?"

Chip nodded. "That's right, Coach." Without waiting for Stone to say anything, he plowed ahead. "Soapy is the person who sent all those letters, E-mails, telegrams, and calls to the NCAA committee."

Stone's eyes widened in surprise. "You're kidding!"

"No, sir. He wired the presidents of A & M and Northern State and Mr. King and just about everyone else he figured could help."

Stone leaned back in his chair and ran his fingers through his hair. "So Soapy Smith was the one," he mused. "What do you know?"

Chip saw the opportunity and continued. "Soapy spent every penny he could get ahold of to finance the campaign, Coach. He spent all he had and even got an advance on his salary to keep it up."

"I knew about the communication barrage to the selection committee," Stone said thoughtfully, "but I never gave Smith a thought. There's no doubt he influenced the committee." Stone was silent for a moment and then continued, "It could be Smith will be responsible for State winning the national championship."

Chip nodded. "I sure hope so."

"Dad Young was telling me about a conversation Ned King had with Tom Merrell. Merrell told King he was getting bunches of letters and telegrams each day and that E-mails were always popping into his inbox from *some* basketball nut in University. Merrell said some of them made sense too."

Stone paused and gave Chip a long look and then nodded knowingly. "You were in on it too," he said. "Right?"

Chip nodded. "Yes, I was, but not nearly as deep as Soapy."

Stone smiled. "You want me to reinstate him."

"Soapy and Rick, Coach. I can straighten them out."

"All right," Stone said. "You take care of it. Tell those two hotheads to shake hands and forget about it."

Chip and his teammates were lined up in the players' aisle waiting to go out on the court for the championship game when West Virginia's jubilant players came off the floor and charged past them. The Mountaineers had won the newly reinstated consolation game. Now they wanted to dress and get back in time to see the start of the big game.

Chip could see the Southwestern University players in the narrow passageway opposite, and he took a deep breath and looked down at the ball, twirling it in his fingertips. His thoughts flew back to the Holiday Invitational Tournament a short three months before. In a few minutes, the result of months of sacrifice and work and trouble would be resolved. Stone touched his arm then and said, "Let's go, Chipper."

The thunder of the crowd was deafening as Chip led the Statesmen out on the floor. He dribbled hard for the basket at the far end of the court and waited with the ball until his teammates formed in three lanes. The cheers of the huge crowd added something to the zip of the Statesmen's passes and shots. They were faultless in the execution of their intricate pregame drill.

The clamor gradually subsided, only to break forth with even greater intensity as the Southwestern players raced to the opposite end of the court. The tall players went right into their pregame show, and the fans roared every time the ball swished down through the net. Twenty minutes later, the buzzer sounded, and the two teams walked to their game benches to wait quietly until the announcer, speaking from the scorers' table, called for silence.

The arena lights were dimmed as the announcer began. "Welcome the challengers, representing the Midwest Conference. All but counted out, this team had what it takes to make a great comeback. The Statesmen won their way to the top of the conference.

"This team is led by an all-America selection who is presently running second in the national scoring race. I give you William 'Chip' Hilton, the captain of State's fighting comeback cagers!"

The big spotlight focused on Chip and followed along as he dribbled the ball to the State hoop, stopping on the ten-second line. The applause was tremendous as he threw the ball back to Dom. The procedure was repeated until all the Statesmen were standing out on the floor. Coach Mike Stone was then introduced. He bowed and acknowledged the applause from his place in front of the State bench.

Now it was the champions' turn. The Southwestern University players were called out one by one as the intense cheering reverberated off the ceiling. Coach Jeff Habley was introduced last. Standing in front of the Southwestern bench, he clasped his hands over his head and shook them in the age-old sign of acceptance of tribute. It was time! The invocation was delivered to a hushed crowd, followed by the singing of the national anthem.

Then the lights came on, with full force, and the cheering crescendo of the crowd strained loudly. The starting players clasped hands with their coaches before walking out to take their positions. The referee moved between Phillips and Bordon and looked inquiringly at the timekeeper. When he nodded, the referee tossed the ball up between the two giants. The championship game was underway.

For a few minutes, the two teams tested each other like two boxers in the first round of a championship fight. Then they opened up. State stuck to the shuffle attack, and SWU relied on its pivot and follow-in power attack. This time, however, State found it difficult to cope with the champions' height. Dom drew three fouls in the first fifteen minutes. Stone benched him for the rest of the half.

Chip was matched against Kinser and played him just as he had the first game. Boxing the SWU star away from the basket had worked before, and it worked again. Kinser got only seven points during the first half. The score at half-time: Southwestern 41, State 39.

During the intermission, Stone and the assistant coaches checked the scorebook while Kelly worked with the players. When the trainer finished, Stone began his talk. "We're getting into trouble with our personal fouls," he said worriedly.

"Dom, Branch, and Rudy each have three personals, and Chip and Jimmy have two. J. C. has four. Half of our team is going to foul out of this game unless we do something about our defense.

"While I was checking the book, I got an idea. I don't know why I didn't think of it before and have it all planned, but I didn't. Anyway, it isn't too late.

"We're going to press them under our basket with our one-two-two zone. If they break through that, we'll hit them with our three-two zone just as they cross the ten-second line.

"If they penetrate the three-two, we'll shift into our two-one-two zone as long as they have the ball in their backcourt. As soon as they move the ball to either side of the court, we go into our one-three-one zone. Got it?"

The players nodded. It was a good plan. No one, but no one, had seen them use the combination all year. Now was the time to spring it.

Stone's jaw was set and his voice was sharp as he continued. "Now for the offense. This half, we're going to give Habley some personal foul trouble of his own to think about. Everyone in this room knows that Chip is a better all-around player than Kinser. It never dawned on me until a few seconds ago that this is the key to winning this game.

"Kinser isn't going to risk fouling out of the game. He wants points, so he'll only do a halfhearted job of guarding. We're going to play some one-on-one basketball, and we're going to start with Chip and let him have the ball every time—as long as it works. I think it will work all right, and if it does and Chip makes fifty or sixty points, all the better.

"If they shift men and put someone else on Chip and Kinser picks up, say, Jimmy, we'll keep it up. Feed the ball to Jimmy and he can use the one-on-one. Remember, when you give the ball to Chip for the one-on-one, clear away from him, go to the other side of the court, and give him room to operate.

"All right! We go back the way we finished, except that Dom goes back in for Tucker. I know this isn't our press team, but it will do as a start to see how SWU reacts. Let's go!"

Phillips passed the ball in to Chip from midcourt to start the second half of the game and the final half of the entire collegiate basketball season. Chip dribbled up the right sideline and over the ten-second line and passed to Dom. Di Santis passed the ball back to Jimmy, who flipped it to Chip and cleared to the other side of the court. Phillips wheeled away, and Chip had the right side of the court all to himself. He faked a shot, and when Kinser left his feet, Chip dribbled around his rival and scored easily.

Polk took the ball out-of-bounds, and the Statesmen put on their one-two-two press. It worked! Jimmy intercepted the ball and scored to put State in front by two points. Again, Polk took the ball out-of-bounds. This time SWU got past the first press but ran into the three-two at the ten-second line, where Chip intercepted. He dribbled all the way to the basket and scored to put State four points ahead, 45-41. A ranting Coach Habley called for a time-out.

When play resumed, the SWU players had their advance worked out, but they weren't prepared for the shift from the two-one-two to the one-three-one, and again the Statesmen intercepted. Chip again scored easily on Kinser.

Coach Habley used all of his time-outs, but he couldn't stop Chip. Kinser was nearly out of control now, playing recklessly in an attempt to hold Chip. He couldn't do it without fouling, however, so Habley took him out of the game for a rest.

The Southwesterners finally got straightened out, and slowly, point by point, they caught up. When Dom drew his fifth personal foul, Mike Stone sent Speed into the game. A few minutes later Jimmy committed his fifth personal. Tucker came in and lasted one play before he was waved to the sideline. Stone took a time-out.

Chip checked the scoreboard. There were four minutes left to play, with State leading by three points, 89-86. Three State regulars had fouled out of the game, but with the exception of Kinser, who was still on the bench, Southwestern hadn't lost a single man by way of the personal foul route. The State lineup was Speed, Bitsy, Branch, Rudy, and Chip.

Time was up and Coach Habley put Sheldon Kinser back in the game. As soon as State brought the ball into the frontcourt, Chip's teammates got the ball to him and cleared out. He faked Kinser out of position and drove around him to score once more. The score was: State 91, Southwestern 86.

Then State fell apart. SWU got past the zones and hit Bordon. The big player pivoted and scored. Branch Phillips committed his fifth personal foul on the play, so Stone sent Rick Hunter in to replace him. Bordon made the free throw to bring SWU within two points of the lead.

Now State led by only two points, 91-89.

Speed took the ball out-of-bounds and passed to Slater, but the tall athlete fumbled. Lloyd picked up the ball, took a one-two dribble, and scored just as Slater fouled him. The big corner man calmly sank the tie-breaking free throw to put Southwestern in front, 92-91.

Chip took the ball out-of-bounds this time and passed to Speed. Then, for the first time, SWU used the press. Speed managed to get into the frontcourt, but Polk stopped him there. Chip looked at the clock. There were just eight seconds!

He called for the ball, but Polk had Speed trapped and forced him to pivot. Speed tried to hook the ball to Chip, but Polk knocked it out-of-bounds. Chip called for a time-out as soon as the official pointed toward the State basket. Only three seconds remained!

When Chip reached the sideline, Stone stood as if paralyzed, looking at the scoreboard. "Three seconds," he murmured. "Three seconds." He turned and grasped Chip's arm. "You'll have to get off a shot. Just catch the ball on the throw-in and put it up."

Just then, Chip saw Soapy peering over Stone's shoulder. He grabbed the redhead and pulled him into the huddle. "Do we have any time-outs left?" he asked Stone.

"Sure!" Stone said. "Two."

"We ought to use them," Chip suggested.

Time was in, then, so Stone walked a few steps away and told the referee he wanted to use up his two time-outs. He came back and looked at Chip. "Have you got a play?"

"I sure have," Chip said. "Soapy's play! He's got a good one, if you put him in the game for Slater."

Stone hesitated only a second. Then he pushed Soapy toward the scorers' table. "Report for Slater," he said.

"*Me?*" Soapy cried.

"Yes, you!" Chip interrupted. "We're going to try *your* play."

"It had better work!" Stone added.

CHAPTER 20

Believing, Hoping, and Trying

SOAPY SMITH was standing on the sideline, and Chip was under the basket, just as they had practiced the play at the YMCA. The Southwestern University players were covering the Statesmen man-to-man, but Bordon had moved back in front of the basket. Kinser stood directly behind Chip. The two all-American stars had Chip sandwiched in between.

The official scanned the playing floor, handed the ball to Soapy, and began his silent count for the throw-in. The redhead faked a pass to the backcourt, then turned and threw the ball toward the State basket. Bordon leaped high in the air, but the ball cleared his hands and hit the board.

Sheldon Kinser saw the ball coming and sensed the play. He sprang forward and crashed into Chip just as the ball came to rest for a split second in Chip's fingertips. The charge knocked Chip off the court, but he had the presence of mind to push the ball back up against the backboard before he went. Just as the buzzer sounded, the ball dropped down through the hoop.

Chip landed out-of-bounds on his feet and looked up at the scoreboard as the lights flashed. There it was: State 93, Southwestern 92.

State had won the national championship!

Chip's teammates had him surrounded and were pulling him toward the sideline when the officials broke it up. "The game isn't over," the referee called. "Hilton has a free throw coming. Kinser fouled him on that last play."

"It's a big point, Chipper," Soapy yelled. "You've gotta make it. Take your time. It's important!"

Chip didn't know what Soapy was making such a fuss about, but he concentrated on the shot. The ball swished down through the net to make the score 94-92. It was all over! State University . . . national champions!

Chip sat on the chair in front of his locker, pulling off his shoes and idly listening to his teammates' celebration and several locker-room guests talking to Dad Young and Coach Stone. All the trouble, headaches, and disappointments were forgotten—the Statesmen fought hard and never gave up. *And what got me through,* Chip thought, *was my faith in God—even during the difficult times—and knowing that God will always be with me.* Then, his thoughts replayed the events following their victory.

The ceremonies after the game took a long time. Chip and his teammates now had their championship watches, and Dad Young had the first national basketball championship trophy State University had ever won. Even now he clutched it as if it were filled with diamonds.

Courtside, the two play-by-play announcers interviewed Chip by the State University bench. They asked him all kinds of questions. Did he know he had scored 47 points and held Kinser to only 19? Had he realized he needed the final free-throw to bring his season total to 950 points to Kinser's 949? Did he know he was the national scoring champion and had the highest game average all locked up?

He had been patient and courteous and answered the questions as best he could. The same kinds of questions were asked of him in the press room. Then it was Soapy's turn.

The redhead had filled Chip's vacant seat beside Coach Mike Stone at the front of the press room, and the reporters began talking to Soapy about his play.

Just before returning to their locker room, Coach Stone broke in and told the reporters how much Soapy Smith had meant to the morale of the team. "Although," he said with a laugh and a wink, "there were times when the redhead was a bit trying."

Chip's reverie was broken when Tom Merrell, chair of the NCAA Selection Committee, came in to the locker room to congratulate the team once more and to ask which player had sent all the letters and messages. "I talked to Dad Young," he explained, "but he couldn't figure it out."

The players looked from one to another, but no one said anything. After a brief silence, Stone said, "The player you are looking for is Soapy Smith."

Merrell shook hands with Soapy. "Those messages must have cost you a fortune," he said. "They were direct and sensible and, in fact, you might say they led the director of the Midwest Conference to wait until a championship was won. We, of course, went along with that decision. Why didn't you sign them?"

"I did!" Soapy said smugly. "Every one of them had my symbol on it, which was just like signing my name."

"I don't follow."

"Well," Soapy explained, "every message had one word misspelled with a double *S* in it, just like a person's initials. The double *S* was for 'Soapy Smith.'"

"That was ingenious enough," Merrell said. "No one could have figured that out."

"No one did!" Soapy said triumphantly, turning to grin at Chip.

"Well," Merrell concluded, "you are to be commended for your persistence. Good luck, men, and congratulations once more."

It quieted down in a few minutes, but Chip remained in front of his locker thinking about Jim Corrigan and Mike Stone. He and his teammates had had a lot going for them this year. Not many players ever got to play for a great coach, much less two . . . and during the same year. Yes, everything did seem to happen for the best . . . if one kept believing and hoping and trying.

• • •

HOME RUN FEUD is an exciting story about the vital importance of teamwork to the game—what State University's captain, William "Chip" Hilton, calls "inside" baseball. Be sure to read *Home Run Feud*—the next exciting baseball adventure in Coach Clair Bee's Chip Hilton Sports series.

Afterword

EARLY IN MY basketball career, I had tremendous encouragement from my parents. Later my high school coach really helped me get ready to take my game to the next level. However, from a very early age, the books in Coach Clair Bee's Chip Hilton Sports Series were a huge motivation for me. Many winter mornings I would be shoveling snow off our court to take a few shots. This after reading another Chip Hilton story the night before.

Clair Bee was one of the all-time great coaches of our game, but he was even more influential to me as the creator of Chip Hilton. Learning how to do things the right way was the message in all of the Chip Hilton books. In an era where winning seems to mean so much, kids today should have the Chip Hilton books as required reading if they want to play high school sports.

I can't wait to share Clair Bee's marvelous stories with my two young sons. I know the books will both teach and inspire them to be better players and, more importantly, better people.

Jim Boeheim
Head Basketball Coach, Syracuse University

Your Score Card

I have
read:

I expect
to read:

____ ____ 1. ***Touchdown Pass:*** The first story in the
series introduces readers to William "Chip"
Hilton and all his friends at Valley Falls High
during an exciting football season.

____ ____ 2. ***Championship Ball:*** With a broken ankle
and an unquenchable spirit, Chip wins the
state basketball championship and an even
greater victory over himself.

____ ____ 3. ***Strike Three!:*** In the hour of his team's
greatest need, Chip Hilton takes to the
mound and puts the Big Reds in line for all-
state honors.

____ ____ 4. ***Clutch Hitter!:*** Chip's summer job at
Mans-field Steel Company gives him a chance
to play baseball on the famous Steelers team
where he uses his head as well as his war
club.

____ ____ 5. ***A Pass and a Prayer:*** Chip's last football
season is a real challenge as conditions for the
Big Reds deteriorate. Somehow he must keep
them together for their coach.

COMEBACK CAGERS

YOUR SCORE CARD

as Chip Hilton and Tamio Saito, competing international athletes, form a friendship based on their desire to be outstanding pitchers. *No-Hitter* is loaded with baseball strategy and drama, and you will find Chip's adventures in colorful, fascinating Asia as riveting as he and his teammates did.

18. *Triple-Threat Trouble:* It's the beginning of football season, and there's already trouble at Camp Sundown! Despite injuries and antagonism, Chip takes time to help a confused high school player make one of the biggest decisions of his life.

19. *Backcourt Ace:* The State University basketball team has a real height problem, and the solution may lie in seven-footer Branch Phillips. But there are complications. Be sure to read how Chip Hilton and his friends combine ingenuity and selfless service to solve a family's and the team's problems.

20. *Buzzer Basket:* State University's basketball team, sparked by Chip Hilton, seems headed for another victorious season. Then, in rapid succession, a series of events threaten to obstruct State's great hopes. Chip Hilton faces some of his most serious challenges and tests of character in yet another book replete with friendship, personal courage, and Clair Bee's exciting basketball action.

21. *Comeback Cagers:* Five fast-moving, hard-fought games leading up to and through the championship game will hold you spellbound. The climax of this action-packed story demonstrates the strength of faith and friendship and involves a startling basketball play! Coach Clair Bee fans will hold their breath in suspense as they read *Comeback Cagers*.

About the Author

CLAIR BEE, who coached football, baseball, and basketball at the collegiate level, is considered one of the greatest basketball coaches of all time—both collegiate and professional. His winning percentage, 82.6, ranks first overall among major college coaches, past or present. His name lives on forever in numerous halls of fame. The Coach Clair Bee and Chip Hilton awards are presented annually at the Basketball Hall of Fame, honoring NCAA Division I college coaches and players for their commitment to education, personal character, and service to others on and off the court. Coach Clair Bee is the author of the twenty-four-volume, best-selling Chip Hilton Sports series, which has influenced many sports and literary notables, including best-selling author John Grisham.